Best Short Stories

Book One

AZ Writers

Granite Publishing

Prescot & Dover

Large Print Edition

Fogarty, Pat: Editor.

ISBN 978-1-7328121-3-0

Prescott & Dover

Large Print Edition

Printed in the United States of America

Original Cover Design by Mariah Sinclair

Cover Photo by Eric Anderson

HBBXN 1551065906

Reviews

—Mike Rothmiller, New York Times Best Selling Author

"Best Short Stories by AZ Writers is an impressive collection of stories written by an eclectic group of Arizona writers. You'll laugh, you'll cry, and more importantly, you'll enjoy the book. The wide-ranging subjects hold your interest and make the reader eager to continue. It's well worth your time."

—Sam Barone, Best Selling Author of the Eskkar Saga Series

This collection of human-interest stories by AZ Writers runs the gamut from humorous to touching to unexpected endings (and some beginnings). Several Stories present poignant childhood memories we all can relate to. You'll also like the editor's choice of quotes from well-known authors. Overall, "Best Short Stories Book One" makes for a well-written and engaging read. It's a very entertaining collection of Short Stories.

Dedication

Best Short Stories Book One is dedicated to the memory of Edgar Allen Poe. & Shirley Jackson. Edgar is considered to be the Father of the American Short Story. And Shirley is considered to be one of the best Short Story Writers of the Twentieth Century.

Also By AZ Writers

Best New Short Stories 2021 Large Print (Nov.2020)
Best Poetry— (Nov. 2018)
Best Short Stories—Book One (Nov. 2018)
Best Short Stories—Book Two (Dec. 2018)
Best Short Stories & More— (Feb. 2019)
Best New Poems— (Nov. 2019)
Best New Poems—(2020)
Best New Short Stories 2019— (Nov. 2019)

Acknowledgments

Without the collective efforts of a fine group of writers, Best Short Stories Book One by AZ Writers would never have become a reality. I would like to thank each author who contributed to this project. A special thanks to Roger Antony, Dan Mazur, Sandy Nelson, Greg Picard, Bill Lynam, Mark Wenden, Bruce Paul & Dennis Royalty for their extra efforts to bring this multi-genre collection to fruition. This compilation of Short Stories began, like most projects do, as an idea.

And, a special thanks to my bride Susan for her organizational skills, common-sense advice, and encouragement.

Pat Fogarty: Compiler, Formatter & Editor

Preface

The Large Print Edition of "Best Short Stories Book One" by AZ Writers contains over 40 captivating stories written by 37 different authors possessing an outstanding range of talent. Unlike many other Short Story collections, in this book, the reader will experience the writing voice and style of many authors. Whereas in most other collections the reader is confronted with a dozen or more stories written by one author who writes stories with the same voice, the same style, and with the same plot, which after a story or two, becomes quite boring. Or, as in many other collections, the reader will find stories written 100 years ago by authors who are no longer with us. In "Best Short Stories Book One" by AZ Writers, the reader will find a contemporary multi-genre collection of stories by dozens of authors who are still, as of this writing, on the green side of the grass. AZ Writers "Best Short Stories Book One" includes memoir stories, historical fiction, creative non-fiction, and many other well-written pieces that will amuse, intrigue, and captivate the reader. A few of these stories may make you laugh, and a few may bring a tear to your eye. In this collection, you will find well-crafted stories with irony, sarcasm, adventure, mystery, crime, and a couple of stories with a bit of romance.

Contents:

Best
Short
Stories
Book One
AZ Writers

Granite Publishing
Prescot & Dover
Large Print Edition

Fire and Snow

Don Martin

THE DAY HAD BEEN GOOD. Lots of new snow, lots of sun, and a good friend made the day exhilarating and enjoyable. George and I had caught the first lift, had stopped for lunch on top, and had finished the day just cruising on the intermediate runs. Our faces were burnt in spots, and brown in others from the sun off the snow. Our legs were tired from skiing and were made heavier by our ski boots. Now it was time to relax, to sit and drink beer, to talk and joke, and to predict the conditions of tomorrow. We sat simply enjoying that feeling that the end of a day of skiing brings.

We sat there in old stiff wooden chairs in front of a huge fireplace crackling and spitting from the wood brought in from the snowbank outside the back door of the bar. This fireplace was large enough to garage my car, and it consumed enough wood in one year to build a football dome. We sat before this roaring dragon of a fire hunched forward staring into the flames with a pitcher and her offspring of two mugs sitting before us on a long low wooden table—a table scarred from decades of abuse from skier's boots and tired legs.

My friend George, and I were avid skiers. George would excuse himself as much as possible from his Volvo dealership in Bellevue to ski. A veteran of well over thirty years of skiing, he could handle any run under any condition. George loved to ski. He was always willing to try a new run or make that extra run at the end of a day. Red and brown from the sun and beer, his bright blue eyes danced beneath his bushy, salt and pepper eyebrows. We sat and relived the day, gesturing with our hands certain turns and jumps that we had made.

The Snorting Elk was filling with the day's skiers and the beer and conversation began to flow. The clomp, clomp, clomp on the wood floor added to the growing din in the "Elk". Soon the tables were all full of skiers; sweaters and jackets hastily discarded and spilling over the backs of the wooden chairs, some on the floor neglected for conversation and beer. It was 1983, and as the volume of skiers increased, so did the smoke from all the cigarettes, hanging a foot or so below the yellowed ceilings that, I swear, had not been cleaned since the day the Elk was built. Not the atmosphere one would find in downtown Seattle. No stress here from lawyers whining about a motion lost, or a deal gone awry.

A crowd had formed around the small bar waiting for their turn for beer, occasionally a skier would turn away from the bar, and clomp, clomp back to his friends, his hands full of mugs and another pitcher of beer, a smile on his face. Today was not any different from any other day on Crystal Mountain, and that full feeling of satisfaction and the glow from the beer began to settle on the crowd.

George and I soon had others flanking us in our perches before the fire. Sharing our long table with other mugs and pitchers, conversations with total strangers began. First a few comments about the day, then a continuous dialogue. This peculiar atmosphere would often lend itself to the sharing of the darkest of secrets with complete strangers. Stories of dark confessions could sometimes be heard at the Elk, however, this day secrets were not the order of the day, quite the contrary, today tall tales soon dominated the conversation, which brings me now to my story.

I had noticed, from early on in the evening, a man sitting next to me on my left, an older heavier fellow. He had sat down earlier with a mug and a grunt. He simply sat and stared into the fire, apparently relaxing and letting conversations float by. Sometimes he would grunt and shift his great bulk in the stiff chair which he sat, and at the same time reach to his mug, take a long swallow, and return the mug to the table. His mug, or what would be left, would land with a thump on the wood table, and his ham of a hand would then disgorge the mug and return to his giant face to wipe away the flecks of foam clinging to his mustache and beard. He was, as I mentioned, a very large fellow, and I noticed that his every movement was followed by a grunt or a snort of sorts. Apparently, any movement required a great expulsion of energy on his part, and I must admit, I wondered how such an individual would ever make it down a ski slope. George had taken absolutely no notice of this great fellow next to me and recited a ski story I'd heard several times before.

Nonetheless, I was delighted at the proportions that this latest version had grown. George was expounding about how changing snow conditions and the effects that sun, at certain times of the day, had on snow. George said, "The effects of morning sun on fresh snow is entirely different from the afternoon sun on old snow. And, as you know, a skier must adapt, not only with the proper wax but also with technique!"

At last, the great fellow sitting to my left began to add to this conversation. "I think, ahem, conditions of this morning, specifically on top, were comparable to conditions at Colorado, or the French Alps." Needless to say, I could not imagine this giant anywhere near the top of Crystal Mountain, not to mention the Colorado, or the "French" Alps.

"Certainly" George replied, "However, we here at Crystal, may only enjoy those conditions for only a few scant hours in a given day, and then perhaps, only for a day or two for an entire season."

George leaned back, the chair creaked, and he shot me a quick glance. He looked at the man next to him and studied him for a moment. The man continued to stare at the fire unmoved by George's inspection.

George asked me, "Carl, would you please pass me the pitcher?".

I handed George the pitcher, handle-first, and he poured beer into the man's mug then into his own. George set the pitcher down and sat back in his chair. The three of us sat and stared into the fire.

"Thank you, my name is David." George said, "You're welcome David. My name is George"

I then offered my hand and said, "My name is Carl, pleased to meet you, David."

"Same here Carl," said David as he shook my hand a couple of times with a firm grip.And after a few seconds of silence, David said, "Ah yes, the Pacific Northwest, I suppose that we all must suffer for the beauty here that surrounds us. A minor thing really, when you add together all that this part of the world has to offer."

George and I looked at each other like 'What is this guy talking about?'

"You're probably wondering what it is that I am talking about," David said. Both George and I were a little afraid to nod our heads in agreement.

"I suppose," David said, "it is the changing conditions here that keeps my attention. What the snow is in the mornings is not what it is in the afternoons. Typically, by afternoon, no matter how perfect the snow may have been that morning, it will become heavy and difficult by afternoon. In fact, the snow can become so heavy by the sun that avalanche conditions can be created in a matter of minutes depending on the angle of the sun, the slope of the mountain, and of course the temperature."

George and I nodded our heads in agreement, like two young executives listening to a CEO's unsolicited bit of wisdom.

The Elk had become very dark by this time as the sun had gone down outside. The fire began to provide light as well as heat to the three of us sitting there. The rest of the skiers in the Elk had begun to quiet down and conversations became muted. Some people had left for home and the dark drive home down the mountain. Others were standing and putting on their cold wet ski gear. A few shuddered as their outstretched arms slid down the sleeves of their damp jackets. As usual, by this time of the early evening, the tables closest to the great wooden front door sat vacant. The Elk was warmer at other tables away from the yawning door. The Elk was certainly far warmer sitting in front of the fire.

In the flickering light of the fire, I watched as Big Dave reached over and helped himself to another mug from our pitcher. George reached down and poured the dregs into his mug. I reached down to the empty pitcher and went to the bar. I sat back down and set the pitcher on the table.

David renewed his conversations on avalanches. "Yes, the avalanche, the bane of all skiers. I have seen men snuffed out like fleas in its white fury." He turned his great head and looked at me, then looked at George. The light of the fire on his face and beard made him look weathered and beaten, his appearance gave his last statement legitimacy. He slowly turned back to the fire.

I could tell that George was affected. Normally George would have either called David's statement bullshit or would have come up with some equally sounding momentous statement. Instead, George stared intently into the fire.

At last, George broke our silence. "I was in Europe, it was January, and I was skiing the French and Italian Alps for two weeks with my fiancé and some friends of ours." George sounded pretty serious all of a sudden.

"We were skiing at St. San Marin. The conditions were perfect. It would snow every night, then sunshine during the day. We took advantage of this and tried to helicopter ski whenever possible. We were having an absolutely wonderful, wonderful, time; endless days of untracked powder, sun, good friends, our youth."

"The hotel packed these huge lunches in big backpacks for us each morning, and at noon we'd find some vista and eat, drink a little wine, it really was great."

"On the fifth morning of this paradise, we were dropped at the top of this one ridge that I can't remember the name of and skied down to the ridge below. We stopped to rest and look around. It was cold and clear, I remember that. We were just standing there chatting when I heard a rumble. I looked over the shoulder of my wife to be and saw that the entire face of snow behind us had started to slide towards us in some weird slow motion."

"There wasn't any time, we all realized that immediately, we were doomed. No one spoke a word, we all turned away and began to ski literally for our lives. I never looked back and I doubt anyone else did either. I'll never know. But, the noise was terrifying, and the wind tremendous. I think that wind, the wind forced ahead of an avalanche, probably bought precious seconds of life for my fiancé and our friends. I think that it contributed to saving my life."

George stopped to drink some beer.

I must admit, I was a little shocked. I'd never heard this story from George before, and I've heard a ton of George's stories. But, I never knew that George had been engaged before Beth, and I'd known the both of them for over fourteen years. There you go, just when you think you know someone.

Big Dave seemed unaffected by George's story. He hadn't stopped looking in the fire since George began. However, he still had some of our beer in his mug. I took a couple hits from my mug. George continued with a guilty lilt to his speech. "I really wasn't the best skier that day, in fact, all the others were better skiers. I was just a little faster."

"I must have reached around 65 to 70 miles per hour, I swear. I've never skied that fast before or since. But I was so scared, not from the speed, all I could hear was this tremendous rumble, my skis felt like brakes, I couldn't ski any faster."

"I didn't notice the cliff until I was right on top of it, not that it really mattered anyway. I just went on over this 50 or 60-foot cliff, only I didn't sail like you see in a James Bond movie, I basically dropped 50 or 60 feet and landed in some deep snow. The base of the cliff was very steep, so I just basically sank into the heavy snow and stopped at the base of this cliff. I immediately got up and climbed back towards the rock face. Just as I reached the rock face the avalanche began to spill over the top of the cliff. I just became one with the rock in hopes that the cliff would offer some protection, kind of like walking behind a waterfall. It didn't take more than a second before I became completely sealed in my snow tomb. I had probably about 18 inches of space between the rock and the edge of the snow and I had ducked underneath a ledge about 2 feet high, so I had enough room to crawl back and forth about six to seven feet at the base of this cliff. I guess I was lucky. I was alive. I'll never know what happened to Ann. They never found a trace of anything."

"But I was as alone as anyone could ever be, and god it was dark."

At this point, George visibly shuttered, and I wished that I could turn on all the lights at the Elk, to help George finish his white nightmare. I was convinced that this story was for real, as never before had George sounded so convincingly honest.

George forged on. "I must have sat there in the dark, in the snow for over an hour collecting my wits before I even moved. Funny how your instinct of survival can kick in and really save your butt. During the whole deal, I still cannot remember ever consciously thinking ' If I am to live.... then, I must do this, then this...' Anyway, I took my pack off and inventoried what I had. I figured I had enough cheese, crackers, apples, and sandwiches to last about three days. Fortunately, or unfortunately, the wine was in one of the other packs."

"You know, I've always believed that if I ever got caught in an avalanche, all I'd have to do is free my arms, dig out enough room to breathe, then dig myself on out.

Simple. But that notion is fantasy, the reality inside an avalanche is very different. What really happens is that once the snow starts to avalanche it almost liquefies due to the heat generated by all the friction and the energy that's released. It kinda turns into a big Slurpee. But when it stops moving, for whatever reason, that Slurpee instantly solidifies, it turns to ice, rock-hard ice. So, I felt around inside my dark ice prison and discovered that exact fact, I was unable to locate any soft spots in the ice."

"I figured that I had two choices. Wait for help to come find me and dig me out. Help was unlikely as the helicopter had set us down miles from nowhere, it would be several hours before anyone noticed that we were missing, and if a rescue party was formed they would wait until light, finally if they waited until light they probably wouldn't come anyway because they'd figure we'd all be dead anyway. Therefore, any rescue effort would not be rushed, they'd take their time looking for our bodies."

"I had to figure out how to survive, number one. Number two, how to survive long enough to dig myself out. As I mentioned before, I figured I had enough food to survive. I was dressed for subzero temps, but not for days at a stretch, but I had nothing to chip the ice with. So, I rummaged around in the dark and discovered that even though I didn't have the wine, I had the wine opener."

"Bravo." said Dave, "But what is a spoon against a mountain?"

George turned to David and said simply "True, but, as they say, I'm here to tell 'ya."

David chuckled, shrugged, and helped himself to yet another slug of our beer.

"As I began to chip at the ice my biggest concern was the spoils from the ice that I'd chipped. I was worried that if the walls of the cavern that I was in were too thick, I'd fill up my little space with ice. Another concern I had was air. With no source of fresh air, I'd likely suffocate. But air was the last of my worries, so I kept on chipping."

"So, I chipped and chipped and chipped and chipped and chipped. I'd chip for about four hours at a whack, then try and sleep or rest for about four hours. At first, every time I'd stop to rest or sleep, I was afraid that I'd never wake up. But I did. I rationed my food in such a manner that I'd only eat once every waking cycle, and then only a few bites. I had no idea how many tons of ice surrounded me, or how long it would take to tunnel to the outside. After what was about two days, I began to weaken, but not fatigue. I was surprised that I was able to survive and at that time I realized that if my food held out, I'd probably make it. By that time I'd probably chipped about ten feet into the ice wall. The cavity that I'd first found myself in had long been filled with the ice tailings. What I was doing was chipping a tunnel moving it along my side with my hands, then kicking the ice behind me with my feet."

"After a time, the tunnel behind me filled with the ice, so I had a space to work in that was about six or seven feet long and barely large enough in circumference for me to work in."

"I can't remember exactly when, but one time when I was chipping I struck something that was not ice. At first, I thought it might be a tree that had gotten caught in the avalanche, but I rapidly realized, to my absolute horror, that I had uncovered a frozen leg of one my companions. I never dug far enough to discover if there was a person attached to that leg, or whose leg it may have been."

"I started to go mad. I'd been in darkness for what seemed an eternity, and then to uncover that leg, well, it was too much. I started to scream. I screamed in desperation, in terrible dark loneliness. I felt totally helpless, that I'd been abandoned by the world and forsaken by God, ignored by Him, left to die in a frozen tomb with the frozen remains of my companions who I began to resent. I resented their fortune at having died so quickly and painlessly while I was forced to suffer in this ice tomb, digging for nothing, digging until I died from exhaustion, or worse, starvation."

"I figured that I'd never get out. So, I stopped and slept. I woke up and just lay there, I decided that if I was to die,

I wanted to die asleep, not digging ice, digging, digging, digging. I was not going to die trying to claw my way to a freedom that did not exist. For all I knew, I had hundreds of feet yet to dig before I got out. I guess I just flat gave up. The hell with it, I thought, I'll just die. So, I went back to sleep, confirmed in my defiance against a pointless death. Comforted against a death that would only come from pointless digging, digging, digging. Assured in knowing that when death came, it would be on my terms, at my choosing, at my time. I was not going to die digging one more inch. So, I slept."

"When I woke up, guess what, I saw light. Not a bright light beckoning me to join my dead relatives and friends in some cosmic group hug, but a faint kind of glow. I knew immediately what it meant, the sun was out, that daylight was out there and that I was close to my freedom. With a renewed strength I attacked the ice. I chipped and clawed and dug and clawed, I took my mittens off and clawed with my fingers and nails, all the while chipping. I was still mad, I started to laugh, first giggling, then laughing outright like the demented. It seemed as if someone else was making all the racket like someone else was in that hole laughing in my face, but it was only me. I was going mad."

"Finally, I punched through. Shafts of the most beautiful golden sunlight began to pop through the hole I was making to the outside. God, it was bright and so beautiful. I stopped once just to let the sun's rays spill on my face. It felt so good. It felt like life was running into my hole giving me strength and energy. The madness left. The laughter had stopped, I was myself again. I finally had a hole large enough to get my arms out of, and I just pulled myself out. I flopped out onto the snow and sunlight. I laid on my back and opened my eyes to the sun burning over my head and stared into the white heat."

George stopped talking and looked into the fire. I looked down at my feet and shuffled my boots around, feeling a little awkward, but really feeling amazed and a little confused that my friend sitting next to me had kept this incredible story inside for so long, and then to let it out in front of a dying fire, and to a total stranger. I felt as if I were the stranger to George, I felt as if I really did not know this friend of so many years, and I wondered why he'd never told me.

Before I said a word, David, the beer bogart decided it was his turn to speak. "That was truly an amazing story my friend. I think that I've never heard another quite like it; however, I have one of my own, that pales in comparison, but I feel compelled to share it with you now." David licked his lips and looked at the empty pitcher of beer, the light from the fire dancing inside. I got the hint and went and got another. When I returned it was obvious that nothing had been said as the two sat staring into the fire. At last David began to speak.

"I have only told this terrible story once or twice since it all happened. It still pains me to think about it, much less relate it to two complete strangers that I'll likely never see again in my life. Yet, what better setting than this to share it, especially following the incredible trial you endured George. Mine is different in many ways, but, death is still the constant, and survival the end."

"I was in France. I was born in France in 1933 and lived there until shortly after the war. I had relatives in England that raised me after the war was over as there was no one left in my immediate family to carry out that responsibility. My family lived in the mountains, in a small village called Vincinces, and had for generations. My father was a carpenter. Anyway, the war came, and we remained relatively untouched by hostilities. Oh, occasionally we'd see airplanes fly over, and the Germans had a small garrison in the valley, but we remained relatively unscathed by the war. At least that was the way it appeared. My father and uncle as I discovered were leaders in the underground, but I never knew that or to what extent until years later. It was their involvement and activities that brought the Germans one day to our house."

"There was a train tunnel at the far end of the valley. It was not a busy train line because the rail line ended on the other side of the mountain in an isolated valley that had even a village smaller than our own. For some reason, the Germans had built something in that valley. Trains began to run with a frequency that was very unusual. The train cars were always closed, sometimes large flat cars would go by with large machinery hidden under great tarps. One day the train entered the tunnel and the tunnel blew up destroying the train. The Germans came in force that day and ransacked our village, several houses were put to the torch, the former inhabitants forced to watch. Of course, the Germans were looking for whomever it was that destroyed their precious train in the tunnel. The violence escalated, several were beaten and tortured in the attempt to discover who was responsible. No one knew who did it, but that did not stop the Germans from their violence. The less the villagers spoke, the more frustrated became the Germans, and the more violent they became. Some men were beaten to death. Two days after the tunnel blew up, a Colonel from the SS arrived to expedite the investigation. He took twenty-five villagers to the town square, tied them all together, doused them in gasoline, and burned them all to death. He announced that twenty-five more would die in the same manner the next day if those responsible did not come forward."

"I'll never know how the Germans discovered that my father and uncle blew the tunnel, but they did. I believe that it may well have been my father, or my uncle, or both that somehow got a message to the Germans that they'd done the tunnel. They could not let more die for their own lives. The Germans came to our house in full force three days after the tunnel to capture my father and uncle. My mother, aunt, and my sisters had left months before to work in factories near Paris. Besides myself, there was only my father, my uncle, and my brother at the farm. The Germans roared up in big trucks. Soldiers spilled from the backs of the trucks running to each side to form a line. The line approached. My father yelled at my brother and me to run to the mountains and not come back until it was safe. We ran to the barn behind the house. We heard gunfire. We ran into the barn and grabbed our skis. The gunfire got louder. We took our skis and ran into the forest behind our farm. The Germans were too busy shooting up the house to notice our escape. There was a trail through the woods that led up to the mountain. I was so scared. I never looked back, I just followed my brother. We started climbing up the mountain and out of the forest. We looked down and saw that our house was on fire and that the Germans had the house surrounded. By the looks of their movements, it was obvious to us that it was over for my father and uncle. My brother urged me to keep moving as it was likely that the Germans would discover our tracks and come after us. I was crying, and my brother told me to stop, that there was time for that later, but that now we had to keep climbing to escape the Germans that were sure to follow."

"We were above the tree line out in open rocks and snow when the Germans spotted us from below. It was a long way down and a few shots were fired in our direction, but none came close. The whistling bullets made us climb faster. We climbed for our lives, our only hope of escape was to reach the top ridgeline and ski down the other side to safety in the forest below. I was confident that given a slight advantage, we could lose the Germans in the large forest on the other side. This forest we both knew very well as we had both spent hours and hours exploring and playing games beneath the green cover."

"Suddenly, the snow around us began to erupt. Small fans of snow jumped around us. Somehow the Germans had caught up to us. I saw my brother throw his arms open wide and he flung his skis into the snow. He fell face down. I saw tiny holes in his jacket. But I could not stop running, I was so scared. The Germans were so close that I could hear the muffled thumps of their boots pushing through the deep snow."

"I finally reached the ridgeline and threw my skis on my feet. Understand, that skis, bindings, and boots were primitive compared to that of today, so it took only a few seconds. Just as I turned to ski down the other side I saw the helmets of two Germans bobbing behind the snow ridge after me. I turned the other way and looked down the other side. To my horror, I realized that I stood over a cliff of some twenty meters and below that the snow started in a very, very steep descent to the edge of the forest. The snowfield from the bottom of the cliff to the edge of the forest was about 1000 meters."

"I looked around trying to figure out another way down when the Germans finally popped up over the ridge and began shooting at me. I had no choice, so I jumped off the cliff, tips down determined to die at the mountain's hand, not by a German bullet."

"I soared down past the face of the cliff about a meter off. All I could see was the snowfield rushing up to meet me. I could hear the popping of the German weapons, but they missed, I guess that I was falling too fast for them to hit me. I knew that once I met the bottom, fell into the snow, that it would be all over, if I managed to survive the fall, in whatever condition it was likely that the Germans would finish me off."

"But the strangest thing happened to me. The snow at the bottom of the cliff was very fresh and very, very light. The wind had blown up the valley all night, so several meters of the absolute lightest snow had piled up at the base of the cliff. It was still very early in the morning and very cold, but the sun was shining. The snow was as light as dust and several meters thick, such a condition is very rare. I dropped in this white fog and kept on going, almost tunneling beneath the surface. I cannot remember for how long, it seemed forever, but I continued my descent through this air light snow. I could not see a thing and I choked and coughed, but I continued on down the hill under a fog-like mist of powdered snow. The Germans could see nothing."

"Finally, I popped through this white dust, this layer of very unique snow, several hundred meters from the base of the cliff, but I dared not stop. The shooting renewed and several bullets came near but not close. I was too far away. I made some turns to throw off their aim and disappeared into the forest and escaped the Germans."

"Incredible!" stammered George. I thought a little too quickly, given the story that I'd just heard from George.

That's when David slowly turned his great head in our direction, his eyes were slightly closed, and he said, "But true."

The Burial

Greg Picard

IT WAS DINNERTIME. I and Ranger Chris Becker were hungry. It had been one of those no lunch days. As the leftover stew from yesterday warmed on the stove, he absentmindedly looked out his kitchen window. The view of the pines and the meadow always soothed him after a long day of struggling with the bureaucracy of being a government employee trying to just do his job. It seemed like more rules came down from headquarters every day. Most weren't thought out well from his perspective.

As the beefy aroma of the warming stew reached him, it set his stomach to grumbling, and with that symphonic backdrop, his kitchen window raised the curtain on a play he hadn't planned on watching.

He watched as two men and a small child walked up the knoll just 30 yards from his cabin. He didn't normally see many folks enjoying the park near his house since there were no trails there. But, that would not have been particularly curious except that one man carried a shovel and the other a large white canvas sack that sagged heavily under the weight of its contents.

“Crap!” He clicked off the burner under the pot and reached for his gun belt that he had laid on the dining room table. He hadn't bothered to take off his entire uniform, only his shirt since he was hungry and, in a hurry, to eat first. He dressed quickly and rather than mess with driving to where they had parked their vehicle, he just stomped out his back door and crossed into the woods just above where they had headed. By the time he got there, the hole they were digging was already a foot deep and two feet across.

“Good grief, you guys dig faster than a hungry badger.”

Both men looked up in surprise, and Chris was taken aback to see tears on the one man who was on his knees next to the hole. Becker rarely had that effect on people until he put handcuffs on them.

"What are you guys..." Becker stopped mid-sentence when the kneeling man moved his leg, and Chris saw the limp Cocker Spaniel laying still on the ground on top of the canvas sack.

"We just came to bury Jack here. He always liked to come to the park, and it is so beautiful here," the standing man said as he stared down at the hole.

"Well guys, that's a bit of a problem. I'm sorry you lost Jack, I really am. You see, we don't allow burials in State

Parks and especially in an area where we have sensitive Native American cultural artifacts and rare natural resources that we are trying to protect.

Great sobs were escaping the one man by now, and Chris noticed the little girl was starting to cry as well. He knew that if parks allowed this kind of thing to go on, people would be burying pets everywhere. The integrity of the resources was at stake, and it just wasn't consistent with the park mission.

Becker looked at the hole. The damage was already done. Nothing essential had been destroyed or unearthed that he could readily see in the late afternoon light. The chill of late fall surrounded them under the pine trees. The forest was in a mood to surrender to the little death of winter only to be reborn next spring as it had for millennia.

No one spoke, and Chris waited a full ten seconds.

"Look, guys, don't ever do this again. Don't tell anyone you did it. It just can't be allowed. I'm going home now, and I'm gonna pretend I never saw you. Don't put up any marker. He reached out and stroked the little girl's hair. She reminded him of when his daughter, Allie, was that age, and her first cat had died from a rattlesnake bite. Some lessons are learned hard. No reason to make them harder now, he thought. It was more than just making "park friends" in the political maelstrom that was California budget allotments. It was more than enforcing the abundance of regulations when people's desires outweighed their good sense brain cells. It was about him being human when he could get away with it.

He turned and walked back to his pot of cold stew. Tomorrow he would make sure the spot was covered with pine needles. Maybe he would dig it up first. Maybe not.

The Thumbprint

Sue Favia

SHE HAD THE BIGGEST HOUSE, the biggest yard, the best food, and a swimming pool in her own back-yard, and of my three aunts, Aunt Doll was my favorite. All our relatives would come to Aunt Dolls and Uncle Joe's house for every holiday and any other occasion that called for food, wine and plenty of beer. But, the most memorable visit was on the Fourth of July.

Neighbors, friends, and relatives all brought their dishes to add to my aunt's dishes, and the entire day was spent eating and swimming. After a few hours of drinking my father and uncles would begin throwing us kids in the pool while my aunts would hover over each one of us making sure we came up for air.

Every time we stepped out of the pool my Aunt Doll would stop one of us kids to go into the house and bring out another utensil or plate of food. The yard was long and narrow, maybe one hundred and fifty feet or more with the house and pool almost at opposite ends of the property.

"Oh, honey, would you bring out that serving fork on the stove and bring me the rest of that sausage in the green bowl," or, "sweetie, there's some more olives in the frig and then grab the block of cheese in the square container on the second shelf on your way out, and put this in the sink on your way in, would ya, Hon," she cheerfully instructed.

My sisters and I made a game about who could get past Aunt Doll without being summoned to bring out another plate of food or carry in an empty one, and then we'd laugh and tease the one who got caught for the next kitchen run.

The food was placed on long banquet tables in the yard near the pool. The cuisine was mostly Italian from the men's side of their family, and Lithuanian cuisine from my aunt's side of their family, in addition to all the traditional American food from neighbors and friends. When the entrees and side dishes were exhausted, and cleared away, the table was once again filled with delicious sweet desserts lasting into the night.

For the entertainment, my Uncle Joe and his friends and neighbors would pool together their firework collections. When the sun fell low in the sky, Uncle Joe and his two brothers would clear a safe place in the yard to set them off. For hours, we would be awestruck, watching the sky dazzle with brilliant streaks of colors and intermittent blasts of cherry bombs and silver salutes. When the fireworks ran out we kids would light sparklers and run through the yard as they flickered in our hands, making circles and figure eights in the night.

Aunt Doll was a large woman with a great presence and a loud contagious laugh, yet another side to her I found to be intimidating. Do as we were told and all was well—cross her and there was trouble to pay.

Aunt Doll was married to my Uncle Joe, my father's younger brother and had six children. Uncle Willie, my father's older brother, was married to Aunt Annie, who also had six children, and the eight of us made twenty, so there was no room for any of us getting away with anything and Aunt Doll cut no slack and played no favorites. She was stern but in a fair and loving way. While she enjoyed us all, she didn't allow misbehavior, disrespect or making a mess in her house. Most of all she didn't allow waste at any meal.

"Take as much as you want," she'd say, "but eat every bite." Her food was the best we'd ever had, and we never left a crumb.

Often in the summer, after one of our warm weather occasions, my cousin Patty and I would plan ahead to stay overnight at Aunt Doll's for a few days, so we could play in the pool and hang out together. Patty was a year younger than I, and the daughter of my Aunt Annie and Uncle Willy.

The pool was above ground, but it was still the biggest and deepest I'd ever seen, in anyone's yard. At my age, I could barely keep my mouth above the water level. I had to stand on my toes and bob up with each inhale to make sure I wouldn't take in any water.

During one of our visits, after playing in the pool all morning with my cousin Patty, my Aunt Doll called us all in for lunch. I had smelled the food coming through the window for the past hour and was starving. Aunt Doll said she was baking ham and she would make us sandwiches for lunch. I believe her entire day was spent in the kitchen, at least through the summer months.

"Time for lunch—come on in. Dry off first, and bring your towels in to sit on," Aunt Doll instructed through the screen door. There was thick-sliced ham with Swiss cheese, potato salad, and for dessert, all the watermelon we could eat. As Aunt Doll passed out the plates to her boys first, Patty and I munched from the bowl of chips on the table. When Aunt Doll set my sandwich in front of me I shuddered at the sight on my plate. There, like a crater, was her large thumbprint, deeply embedded in the soft white bread.

I sat at the table staring at it in dismay, contemplating my options. This was definitely going to be a problem. There was no way I could eat that thumbprint.

I began with the undamaged half of the sandwich, then I ate the potato salad and chips. I knew the watermelon would have to wait. I had to approach the other half of the sandwich with careful consideration.

Slowly and systematically, I began eating my way around the oversized thumbprint, avoiding the depressed area completely, thinking I could dump the contaminated portion in the garbage when my aunt left the room. But, no such luck, Aunt Doll was having more company over for dinner that night and had a pot of spaghetti sauce cooking on one burner and another pan of sausage and green peppers on the other. She wasn't leaving that stove, not for a minute.

"You kids need to finish up here, I've got to get started on my Jello molds and I need the table." Aunt Doll said.

Aunt Doll was the queen of Jello molds. Whenever there was a family gathering, she would make her famous fresh fruit creation, mixed with cream cheese and strawberries, sometimes pineapple or orange segments, stacked high with fresh whipped cream.

My cousin Patty was making great strides with her lunch, and Aunt Doll's two older boys were already finished and running out the back door to the pool again.

"Hey, Jodie, get back here," she yelled, as the door slammed behind him. "I said finish everything—and that means your milk, too." Jodie ran back in, chugged down the rest of his milk losing much of it down his bare chest, and almost in the same sweep, scrambled back out the door to beat his little brother Mark to the pool.

Patty and I sat at the table, as my aunt, all too often, glanced at our plates. As my sandwich was getting smaller and smaller, it seemed as if the thumbprint was getting bigger and bigger. If she forced me to eat it, I knew I would gag, or possibly worse. I'd never be able to come back again—ever. My mother once forced me to drink the rest of my 7-Up after I allowed some birthday cake to back-wash into the last remaining few inches of the bottle. I gave a warning signal with some gag reflexes which, unheeded, led to the entire contents of the pop, cake, and recent lunch ending up on the floor. The thumbprint had inevitable possibilities. I couldn't bear the humiliation, but even more, Aunt Doll being angry with me. Would she understand? Would she know it was about her thumbprint?

I knew this was not normal. It's not like I saw her lick her fingers or pick her nose. At home, whenever my mother left an imprint in my food, all I had to do was remove it from my plate and drop it on the floor and Blackie would take care of the rest. With ten of us at the table, who would notice anyway? But Aunt Doll did not have a dog and it was only Patti and me sitting at the table. I couldn't tell Patty about the thumbprint, she'd think I was crazy—nor would she understand—I'm not sure I did.

I sat there, now, looking at the circular mound on my plate, nibbling as close as was safe to the edges of the imprint, so it wouldn't appear so large.

Patti had finished and was nudging me to hurry up, we could both see that our aunt was becoming impatient. The longer I stalled, the more attention was drawn to the thumbprint that was now beginning to look like the size of a hubcap.

Patty stood up and stared at the odd remnant on my plate, then Aunt Doll turned around looking at my plate as well. The two of them stood there watching with puckered eyebrows as if it were a science project and they were waiting for it to move.

It seemed as if time stopped—as well as my breath. Tears welled up and rolled down my face as I sat in my anxiety. Without turning her head, my aunt somberly said to Patty,

"Now you go on outside and play, hon," she said, with her eyes still fixed on my plate.

Oh, my god, she wanted no witness. I wanted to yell to Patti, "don't go—stay outside the screen door."

Now, I envisioned myself on the floor in a half-nelson, with Aunt Doll prying my mouth open to force-feed me this vile mutation of what had seemed like, a lifetime ago, just a sandwich. I had just learned in school that the human jaw was the strongest muscle in the body—so even given the size of her hands, I knew there was a good chance that if I didn't scream, nothing was going into my mouth. I was shocked out of my vision as her large hand reached over my shoulder, picked up my plate, and allowed the thumbprint to slide into the trash.

As she gave me a half-wink and nudged me out the back door I thought I almost saw the corners of her mouth ever so slightly turn up.

Irish Resentments

John Maher

THE IRISH ARE NOTORIOUS for holding their resentments. Just study Irish history and that green land's 800-year resistance to the English occupiers. The Irish rebelled and lost fifteen times until they won their freedom in 1922. The Irish don't stew, plot revenge, or carry on vendettas. We're pragmatic. We wait because we know that what goes around comes around. We don't forget. As Robert F. Kennedy, one of America's most prominent Irish-Americans once stated, "Don't get mad. Get even."

In 1920, when my father was ten years old, and head altar boy at St. Michael's Roman Catholic Church in Flushing, New York, a young priest arrived from Ireland as a new member of the parish's clerical contingent. He was "Lace Curtain Irish," meaning his people were property-rich in Ireland. Most of the Irish parishioners of St. Michael's came from "Shanty Irish" stock. Their people had been "dirt-poor" tenant farmers in Ireland. These parishioners regarded The New Priest with measured contempt. His custom-tailored black priest suits, his own personal altar vestments, his ornate gold chalice, and his aloof persona heightened their disdain.

But it was the pride he had for a book that heightened their animosity. The book was his special Missal, the liturgical volume encompassing the words and gospels a priest uses to celebrate Mass. Pope Pius XI himself in Rome had blessed this special Missal, and The New Priest acted as if its glorious status added to his self-importance.

The New Priest's Missal was a prodigious book with a sumptuous tooled leather cover and binding, gold embossed lettering, rich illustrations, and parchment pages. Many St. Michael's parishioners quipped that it wasn't a Missal at all; it was a reproduction of the Book of Kells, the famous 1,200-year-old Irish manuscript displayed at Trinity College in Dublin. The Missal was maybe a foot thick and weighed approximately twenty pounds. The New Priest venerated his special, Pope-in-Rome-blessed Missal. To many of his parishioners, he had greater esteem for his book than his flock.

Every Sunday, in keeping with his head altar boy position, my father served the main 10 o'clock mass. A bulk of parishioners attended this mass weekly, including my devout grandmother, Nana. Born and raised in County Limerick, Ireland, she immigrated to America in the late 1890s, another one of the boatloads of Irish girls used as domestics. As she did every Sunday, she sat in the second pew on the right. She was there not only to pray and celebrate the mass but to gaze with joy as her oldest child, and firstborn son served mass, in her judgment a harbinger for what she believed would be his destiny as a priest. Shortly after The New Priest's arrival, he said the 10 o'clock Sunday mass for the first time.

At the appointed time in the mass, the altar boy moves the Missal from the left side of the altar to the right. As my father commenced doing this, hugging the immense book to his ten-year-old chest while negotiating the maneuver, he stumbled on the hem of his oversized black cassock; the ankle-length clerical robe altar boys wear under the white surplice. And he tumbled headlong down the three steps and off the altar. He landed in a heap on the marble floor just inside the altar rail. The Missal arrived nearby a millisecond later with a resounding *splat*.

At the explosion of the Missal landing, the priest halted mass. He turned on his heel, looked over the wreckage that had unfolded below him, and bolted down the three steps towards my father sprawled on the marble floor. Everyone in the church assumed he intended to minister to my father's possible injuries. Instead, he seized my father by the arm, jerked him to his feet, and smacked him in the back of the head with a vicious roundhouse right. The *thwack* echoed throughout the church.

Then, the priest went over to his special Missal and gathered it, and its brass stand off the marble floor. Caressing it to his bosom as if it were a mistreated puppy, he carried it back up the three steps to the altar. He ignored my father still standing dazed by the altar rail. Once positioned again at the head of the altar, he tenderly set the Missal and brass stand on the right-hand side. Then with indifference, he returned to the mass as if nothing had taken place. Dead silence permeated the church.

In the second pew right-hand side, my Nana's piercing blue eyes scrutinized the goings-on with seething fury. Because she held clerics in the highest esteem as required of a good, respectful Irish-Catholic, she said nothing to the priest then or ever regarding his mistreatment of her child. But from that moment on, she seldom spoke to the priest. She avoided any dealings with him if possible, and never allowed him to hear her confession, always going to one of the other priests for her weekly visits to the confessional. This occurrence led to two developments, one two hours afterward, the other in thirty-five years.

At roughly high noon on that Sunday in 1920, after my father had completed his chores as head altar boy, he withdrew The New Priest's special, Pope-blessed Missal from the sacristy, the place where clerics and altar boys assemble for mass. Cradling the twenty-pound book in his arms, he plodded up the six flights to the top of St. Michael's belfry. Once there, he opened a small access door in the belfry that faced onto Union Street, one of the major avenues in Flushing. Then, he threw the Missal out into the open waiting air. It sailed fifty feet to the pavement below, where on impact it exploded like an IED, albeit a holy one. The book's spine snapped in several places, scattering its parchment pages over Union Street. My father suffered no guilt in doing this. In fact, he felt quite satisfied.

Thirty-five years later, on a hot, muggy July 1955 Sunday morning, my Nana walked the half mile from her home on Avery Avenue to St. Michael's Roman Catholic Church. As she had every Sunday for fifty years, she would attend the main 10 o'clock mass. At seventy-five years of age, she was built like a small draft horse, short, thick, boxy. She wore a Navy-blue rayon dress with a string of pearls around her neck. A matching blue pillbox hat with a veil nested on her head. Black Oxford shoes with squat heels squeezed her swollen feet. Midway up the front entrance to the church doors, her heart gave out, and she collapsed on her back there on the steps.

Concerned parishioners gathered around her. The New Priest, now The Monsignor and head of St. Michael's, happened to be present. His routine every Sunday demanded he receive his flock in his custom-tailored black priest suit and spit-polished brogans to glad-hand or browbeat them as they attended mass. He rushed to my Nana's side and kneeling asked, "Nellie, do you need The Last Rites?"

My pious grandmother, though dying, drilled her piercing blue eyes into the eyes of this man she had despised for thirty-five years and said, "Not you, ya bastard." She glanced up at the crowd hovering near her and said, "Get me another one." The priest who was to celebrate the 10 o'clock mass was called from the sacristy. He arrived flustered in full liturgical regalia, along with a flock of nervous altar boys also dressed to serve mass. He knelt on the steps and gave my grandmother The Last Rites. And then Nana died.

**This story is a tribute to my grandmother and my father. It illustrates my belief that much of who we are and what we are is the product of the people who came before us. I carry and cherish the spirit of my father and my grandmother*

All Quiet on the Bureaucratic Front

Dan Dražen Mazur

PETER WAS A QUIET MAN living in a quiet neighborhood in a quiet town. Life was quiet but a bit boring. He had no relatives, no family of his own, no friends and no pets. The only thing he had going for himself was his work, and now this has changed as well because his company was downsizing. For years he worked as a salesperson at a stationary store of a neighboring town, traveling every day back and forth about thirty miles each way. There, Peter was appreciated because he seldom complained about crazy scheduling. He agreed to work weekends, afternoons, and he was available to fill in on short notice. He was taken for granted a bit and taken advantage of a lot. However, seniority made Peter the highest-earning salesperson on the floor, and the company would save money by letting him go. He was replaced with two entry-level part-timers.

The new situation hit Peter quite hard and he spent a week in quiet desperation, and then picked himself up and made a few weak attempts to find another job, to no avail. The economy was not at its highest, and Peter was too old and quiet, so someone would always beat him, either by being younger, having better credentials, or leaving a better job interview impression.

Peter gradually became depressed, and after thinking of different options, decided to commit suicide. Peter, being who he was, choose a different pathway of departure, from what many other, serious, committed suicide candidates would do: after selecting when's, where's, and how's to do it, then writing a goodbye letter, be on their way by jumping from a bridge, laying down on railroad tracks, hanging or shooting themselves, or simply overdosing on a bunch of over-the-counter sleeping pills. No, Peter was too quiet, too mild, too modest, and much too law-abiding citizen. He knew that taking one's own life was not permissible, and to make it legal he decided to get a permit to do it.

So, Peter went to the county Public Works Department and waited his turn for a prolonged time. He then approached the clerk there, inquiring about the paperwork for a permit to commit suicide. The clerk said they had no such forms and directed him to the Department of Public Safety in the State government office building. The State building was in a neighboring town, where Peter used to work, and Peter postponed his visit to the next day. He drove there the following morning, only to be told that such forms are not available there either, this could likely be a federal matter. He was told to address his issue to the GSA department, which stood for General Services Administration. Luckily, the federal building was close by, and after waiting for employees to come back from an hour and a half long lunch, he was told that there was no specific form for his request. The clerk there was very nice and suggested he should write a letter of request, but to submit it to the county government. The courteous federal government clerk went further and continued that he should be prepared to wait for their response because they were swamped with high-priority cases, and short on personnel, which is why she recently switched jobs from there and came to work for the federal government. The county situation was crazy, and she was much more relaxed now.

Peter agreed and drew up a letter of request on his computer. He couldn't print the letter right away and had to go back to the stationary store he used to work in, where he was greeted by his fellow worker and store manager. He needed to purchase a Magenta ink cartridge for his printer. Oddly, his printer wouldn't print in black ink, although there was plenty of black left in its respective cartridge, but the Magenta ink cartridge was empty, and there you have it. Color cartridges were expensive, and Peter figured out this was a way the cartridge makers were cleverly but unfairly making extra money.

When the letter was printed and looked good enough for submission, Peter decided to avoid a long wait in line and sent it through the regular mail. He kept a copy of the letter, frequently reading it, and found that several improvements could be made to it, but it was too late. The letter was entitled, To Whom It Might Concern, and titled Request for a Permit to Commit Suicide.

Several weeks passed by, and finally, Peter got the notification that his *Request* was denied due to failure to pay a filing fee. The letter did not specify the amount of the filing fee, and Peter went there in person where he discovered, after a nominal waiting time, that not only filing fees need to be paid, but also penalty fees for non-compliance. The amounts for both were not too bad, but they accepted only cash or official checks. The clerk kindly explained that credit cards were not accepted because credit card companies take a chunk of every transaction, which lowers the amount left for the county. As far as personal checks were concerned, there were too many bounced checks in the past, and it was a nightmare to collect the monies again, including the fees that the bank charged for bounced checks.

Peter went to an ATM and withdrew cash, returning to the office. After waiting some more, Peter realized that there was another clerk there. Since Peter had not brought their letter, this nitpicky clerk couldn't identify the case without the number they'd assigned to it. The fact that earlier the different clerk had no problem locating Peter's case without any letters and numbers didn't help. So, Peter had to drive back home to get that letter. All this driving back and forth was quite exhausting, and Peter became mildly irritated and tired of this runaround.

He was mildly speeding, trying to get back to the county office before closing time, and wouldn't you know it, he was stopped by the police and given a speeding ticket. This put Peter in a bad mood, and when he arrived at the County Clerk's office, he was already irritated with the situation and was kind of short with that clerk, who found Peter's behavior less friendly and less submissive than he was used to. The clerk immediately took it personally and took a defensive posture. He was agitated with such aggressive customer behavior and refused to offer any help with Peter's request.

Consequently, Peter's stamped, and fees-paid request wound up at the bottom of a huge paper pile. Peter feared it would take a while for his request to be considered. The clerk was exulted for not telling Peter that in case of the address change he should report it within ten days, otherwise if the post office returned their mail with the Permit, there would be no attempt to locate the party's in question current address.

Peter didn't know that and indeed moved to a cheaper place. He failed to report the new address within ten days. He waited and waited, and little by little got used to being in limbo for so long. He even quietly began enjoying life, food stamps, and other conveniences the government provided to poor people. He even started quietly singing when taking a shower. Life was good, and Peter looked forward to living a long and happy quiet life before receiving the government's Permit to Commit Suicide, if at all.

Respecting Bees

Mark Wenden

I WAS KNEELING IN THE DRIVEWAY in front of my parent's garage putting clean grease on the chain of my 3-speed Schwinn Racer when the tedium of the lazy Midwestern summer afternoon was broken by shouts in loud, angry Russian. I looked up in surprise to see our next-door neighbor shirtless in his backyard, dancing about and slapping himself, and barking out phrases. "…tvoyu mat'! Chornyi blyad! Chort vozmi!" which had to be horrible curses. His lawnmower, still running, stood abandoned. As I gaped at him uselessly, he eventually stopped the swatting, killed the engine of his mower, and approached the fence. He had lived next door for about a year, and I did not know him well. To me, he looked old, though he probably was only in his fifties. He was quiet and seemed to always move in a deliberate way, wasting no motions. He always had a weary look about him.Resting a hand on the fence he asked me, in his slow, accented English, whether we had any baking soda in our kitchen, and if so, could he use some to make a plaster, as he had just been stung by yellow jackets (which he called bees) whose underground nest had been disturbed by his lawnmower. I told him I would look, and he asked me to bring whatever I found over to his kitchen.

As I rummaged through my mother's cabinets, it struck me how odd it was that this man had crossed half the world to be stung by yellow jackets in a backyard in Ohio. The word in the neighborhood was that he had served in the Red Army during World War II and survived heavy fighting during the German invasion. Then, as a reward for his heroism, he was convicted on trumped-up charges of collaboration with the enemy and thrown into a labor camp for ten years. Surviving even that, after his release, he defected from the Soviet Union by swimming to Finland where it borders Russia on the Baltic Sea. He applied to be permitted to immigrate to the US. Before the war, he had worked as a civil engineer. Possessing such useful skills, and with Cold War sentiments being on his side as well, permission was granted. He arrived in the US in the late fifties and worked menial jobs until his English was good enough to apply for work in his profession. He lived alone, and no one knew what had become of his family.

Having found a box of baking soda, I trotted over to his back door and he waved me into his kitchen. He carefully mixed the soda with water in a bowl and dabbed the paste onto the angry-looking stings with the back of a spoon. He was mostly silent, occasionally sucking some air through his teeth and muttering. He did not seem to mind that I stayed and watched. Perhaps he didn't want me to leave with the baking soda in case he needed more.

When he had applied plaster to all the stings, and I counted more than ten, he went to his garage, where I heard things being knocked about on a shelf. He then emerged into the yard with a can of insect spray. He thoroughly doused the opening of the yellow jackets' nest and sent a good long stream of insecticide down the hole. He came back inside and threw the empty can in the trash.

"I hate bees too!" I said, wishing to show that I sympathized with him for the pain the stings must be causing him.

"Who said I hate bees?" he answered in his carefully enunciated way (Khu sayt I hett biss?). He sat down at the kitchen table opposite me and gave me a look that meant, I knew immediately, that he wanted to say something he considered important.

"Actually, I respect bees. The bees which sting-ged me were only defending their home. I feel they have every right to do this, and I admire their self-sacrifice and the singleness of their purpose. They did not hesitate to fly out and attack me, though I am many times larger than they, and my lawnmower must have been terrifying as it passed over their nest."

He raised a finger. "Where I grew up, in addition to many kinds of bees, there are other animals such as bears and wolves, which can easily kill men. I never hated them for this ability, but learned to respect them, to stay out of their way and not disturb them." I felt puzzled by this short talk of his. It was the longest I had ever heard him speak at one time, and replied, "But didn't you just walk out there and wipe out their nest with bug spray?"

"Yes!" he exclaimed. Then he leaned toward me and fixed me with an intense look. "This is what you must understand, boy. I do not hate them for being what they are. And I even admire some of their finer qualities. But if they attack me, they are making a tragic mistake. I will kill every last god damn one." I saw the gleam of a gold tooth as a tight smile slowly cracked his face. His expression relaxed, and his eyes crinkled slightly in amusement as he registered my surprise, both at his language and at what seemed to me, at my age, to be self-contradictory thinking. He patted me on the shoulder and thanked me for the baking soda.

It wasn't until years later, in a world history course at Ohio State University, that something reminded me of this conversation, and I realized he had been talking about much more than bees.

The beginning is the word and the end is silence. And in between are all the stories.
—Kate Atkinson

Maynard Franklin's Passing

Roger Antony

I RECEIVED A TELEPHONE CALL this past Monday from a man named Edward Cushing, who introduced himself as Uncle Maynard's attorney. He called to tell me that my uncle had passed away on Saturday at his home and that I should attend the reading of his Will in his Phoenix office on Thursday at 11:00 a.m.

Edward said that Uncle Maynard had written in the latest amendment to his Will that only his two nephews and niece should be present.

Maynard was one of my mother's two brothers. Her brother Tobias, seven years younger than Maynard, has been in declining health for several years. The last time I saw Tobias was at a family gathering at Maynard's house on Camelback Mountain six years ago. Tobias came with his wife Margaret, son Tom, and daughter Lucy.

On Thursday morning, I took the express elevator to the attorney's office on the eighteenth floor of the North Tower Plaza in central Phoenix. In less than a minute, I stood facing the Killingworth, Cushing, and Roberts law firm receptionist, an attractive blond-haired woman who welcomed me to their offices, asked my name then gestured to their waiting area where Tom and Lucy Franklin were sitting.

Tom, an accountant with a local concrete supplier, rose and greeted me. He was tall, thin, and wore glasses like his father. His sister Lucy, an eighth-grade English teacher in the Glendale school system, sitting opposite him on a leather sofa also stood. She wore her auburn hair tied in a bun making her look older and more uptight than her brother. We shook hands as if we were business acquaintances, not family, and offered apologies for failing to keep in touch. Tom relayed that their father was in a nursing home in Sun City and their mother was living nearby in an apartment.

A few minutes after eleven o'clock a woman in her mid-thirties wearing low heels, a pinned striped black business suit with a red ascot approached us, told us her name was Marian, and asked that we accompany her. We walked past several rooms with etched glass doors before she opened the door to a spacious corner conference room with floor-to-ceiling windows providing unobstructed views to the west and north.

Before leaving us, she asked if we would like something to drink. In unison, we replied, "coffee."

While we waited for Marian to return, we stood shoulder to shoulder and stared out the north-facing windows. It was another cloudless fall day and we could almost see Uncle Maynard's house on Camelback Mountain through a faint brown haze of smog.

Marian returned to the room a few minutes later with a silver tray containing a carafe of coffee and five glass mugs. She laid the tray down and then left the room, returning a minute later with a second silver tray. This tray contained an assortment of pastries and bagels. From a small refrigerator built into the maple credenza that matched the south and east paneled walls, she retrieved a container of butter, a small carton of cream, and a container of strawberry cream cheese.

Before leaving us she said, "Mr. Cushing is on the phone. He will be with you in a few minutes. Call if there is anything you need. My extension is 53."

My bagel was warm and delicious with a light coating of strawberry cream cheese. The coffee tasted like Starbuck's French Roast. I was standing by the carafe refilling my cup when the etched glass door opened and a man in his early forties with neatly trimmed jet-black hair stepped in. He wore horned rim glasses and a nicely tailored suit that did a good job of concealing his weight.

He introduced himself as Edward Cushing and quickly shook hands with Lucy, Tom and me. I was the furthest from the door, so I was last to receive his proffered hand.

In his left hand, he held a thick manila folder bound with a rubber band. Placing the folder down at the end of the table, he stepped to the refreshments on the credenza, drained the carafe, and added two packets of sugar before picking up the telephone. He pushed several buttons then spoke into the mouthpiece. "Marian, would you bring us a coffee refill?"

On his way back to the folder, he glanced appreciatively out the expansive floor to ceiling windows and said, "What a view."

He placed his coffee mug next to the folder, sat down and slid off the rubber band removing four sets of stapled papers. He handed one set of papers to each of us. At the top of the first sheet in big scrolled letters were the words, Last Will and Testament. Beneath the heading, the first line began with, "I, Maynard Franklin, being of sound mind."

I began reading and was on the third line when Edward Cushing cleared his throat and said, "Each of you has a copy of Maynard Franklin's Last Will and Testament. Mr. Franklin revisited his Will several times in the past year. The copy before you is his last recorded Will. He amended it on October sixteenth, ten days ago."

"Do you have any questions before I proceed?" asked Edward.

I looked to Lucy and Tom seated across from me. Neither appeared prepared to ask a question, so I did. "Mr. Cushing, will there be a funeral service for my uncle?"

"Per his instructions, there will be no funeral service."

"Do you know why?" I asked.

"Mr. Franklin did not want a funeral. His instructions are found on the last page of the stapled document before you."

I turned to the last page. Sure enough, my uncle had stated that he did not want an announcement in the newspaper or a funeral. He further stated that he wanted his body cremated and his ashes scattered in the Superstition Mountains. When I finished reading my uncle's latest codicil, I looked up to find that Tom and Lucy were still reading. I turned to Edward, who was trying to judge whether to start talking or to wait for Tom and Lucy to finish. A few moments later they both looked up.

Tom and Lucy stared at me as if I might be able to offer some insight into our uncle's actions. I gave a slight shrug then turned to Edward, who cleared his throat.

"Any questions?" he asked.

Tom and I shook our heads. Lucy said, "No."

Edward began reading the Will, "I, Maynard…"

According to my mother, Maynard had been the student in their family and the most ambitious. Her brother, Tobias, tried but never could match Maynard either as a student or in his career. She said that Tobias being the youngest in the family had suffered from the birth order syndrome. He was the least bright, the least ambitious and the least athletic in the family. In contrast, Maynard excelled at everything.

After graduating as valedictorian from college, Uncle Maynard played professional football with the Oakland Raiders for seven years before retiring from the NFL, returning to Phoenix and purchasing a small automobile dealership. He later bought three more dealerships and at the age of fifty was owner and CEO of four automobile dealerships in the Phoenix area. When he turned sixty-nine, he sold them to AutoNation, the automobile conglomerate.

My father worked as a lineman for Arizona Public Service, the local electric utility, and my mother worked as a nurse at Baptist Hospital. After a drunk driver killed my father, Uncle Maynard offered to pay for my college education. It took a big burden off my mother's shoulders, but she insisted that I could not accept my uncle's offer unless I worked for the money. As a result, I worked at one of his dealerships during the summers and on weekends throughout high school and college.

Maynard and his wife had no children. My mother always suspected that her older brother was too busy to raise kids and was content to lavish gifts on his nephews and niece.

Edward's baritone voice faded into the background as I reminisced. Moments later, I looked up to find Tom staring at me and realized that Edward was reading from page two of the Will, so I quickly turned the page. Just as quickly, another memory of Maynard and his wife appeared.

My parents rented an eight-person houseboat at Lake Powell for four days when I was in middle school. They made the reservation in early February for the first week in August and invited Uncle Maynard and his wife, Tobias and his family.

It was only the second time I had been to Lake Powell. After that, I visited the Lake at least once a summer. Ultimately, the Lake and the area were too inviting and when Elsie and I married, we decided to make Page our home.

On the houseboat trip, Tom and I were responsible for carrying the boxes of food and supplies from our cars to the houseboat. Just before we departed, Uncle Maynard told my father that we needed to stop at the marina. Unbeknownst to my parents, Uncle Maynard had rented two powerboats for the four-day outing so we could explore the small canyons inaccessible to the houseboat.

I spent much of my time during the trip in a powerboat. Once again, my uncle surprised us and made a great vacation even better.

When my mother and father were planning the trip, they considered a powerboat but decided against it because of cost. Cost never seemed to be an issue with Uncle Maynard. He was always intent on making the most of his time. He certainly made my vacation and I thanked him profusely when we landed back at Wahweap Lodge. As usual, he just smiled and said he was glad I enjoyed it.

The next moment I found myself back in the conference room with Tom and Lucy staring wide-eyed at me with a look of disbelief. Lucy's normally erect posture had crumbled, and her mouth sagged.

I looked to my left and saw Edward staring at me. I blinked a couple of times then shifted my gaze back to Tom whose hands now covered his eyes, his head bowed forward. Immediately, I knew that I had missed something terribly important in the reading, so I looked to the attorney.

Edward looked at me then asked, "Do you want me to continue?"

Nearly ten seconds passed before Tom looked up and, in a voice barely audible said, "Give me a minute, please."

Edward said, "Take as much time as you need. I'll let you talk among yourselves." He stood up and opened the door. Before leaving he said, "When you're ready, call Marian or stop at the receptionist's desk."

Tom nodded then lowered his head while Lucy and I watched Edward depart. The room was silent for several minutes before Tom raised his head, cleared his throat and spoke. "I can't believe Uncle Maynard would do that."

Lucy added her tone seething with contempt, "He was manipulated."

"What?" I said, "Weren't you listening? He gave his entire fortune to his arts foundation. We get nothing, nothing at all," Lucy said.

"Oh," I said. It was evident that Tom and Lucy expected to receive a portion of Uncle Maynard's wealth upon his death. Apparently, his decision to establish and fund an arts foundation precluded any inheritance.

My uncle's actions did not surprise me since he had been a benefactor for various arts groups and charitable organizations throughout his working years. Several times, he headed the Phoenix Chapter of the United Way and was one of their largest contributors.

Elsie and I had talked about my uncle on Monday evening. I explained to her that he had been a very special person to me: helping my mother after my father died, helping me financially to go to college and always giving meaningful gifts. It sometimes upset my parents knowing that my childless uncle's presents were always more sensible and insightful than theirs. As a result, I opened up his birthday and Christmas presents last, having learned that you always saved the best for last.

Uncle Maynard's practice of giving thoughtful gifts continued with our son who looked forward to his great uncle's gifts. Somehow Uncle Maynard knew exactly what a child wanted at every age and somehow always found that special gift. My uncle had been much like Ebenezer Scrooge helping Tiny Tim after the visitation by the third spirit in Charles Dickens' *Christmas Carol.*

"He gave his whole damn estate to charity," said Tom, "his whole fortune."

I responded, "It was his money. It was his choice."

"Don't you understand," said Lucy. "We are family. We should have inherited the money."

"Lucy, Uncle Maynard was very generous to us during his lifetime. We should be thankful," I said.

"Thankful for what?" said Lucy. "He was a senile old man. The lawyer probably convinced him to give away his money." Turning to her brother, she said, "We should contest the Will. He obviously wasn't of sound mind."

Tom looked at me and asked, "Todd, do you agree?"

"Tom, it was Uncle Maynard's choice. The money will help many people in the Phoenix area. I think he wanted to leave a legacy of goodwill."

"So, you think he was sane?" he asked.

"I think he wanted to give back to the community where he made his money. We all have jobs. We can get along without his money," I said. "You're an editor of an obscure newspaper in Page. Don't you want a new house, a new car, a boat, a vacation home and do some traveling?" asked Lucy.

"No," I said."You're a fool," said Tom. "We should have gotten something."

"We did. He gave us his love and his generosity while he was alive. That should be enough. Why should we expect more?"

Turning to his sister Tom said, "I've had it. I'm going to get a lawyer and fight this."

"I agree," said Lucy.

They rose from the table in unison and without saying goodbye left the room. A few minutes later Edward Cushing opened the door. His face did not reveal any surprise or concern given that two of the three people called to the reading of Maynard Franklin's Will had left in a huff and were contemplating legal action against his law firm and their uncle's Will.

Still standing Edward asked, "Are you comfortable with your uncle's decision to leave his entire estate to the Franklin Arts Foundation?"

"If that's what my uncle wanted, then I see no reason to dispute his actions," I said.

"Are you sure? Your cousins don't share your opinion," he said.

"I know. They expected to benefit from our uncle's passing."

"Todd aren't you a bit disappointed?"

I said, "My uncle was very generous to me growing up and has been generous to my son. He was an extraordinary man. I am going to miss him. I am comfortable with his Will."

"Good. I'm glad to hear that."

A moment later, there was a soft knock on the etched glass door. Marian opened it just enough to see Edward. When Edward nodded his head, Marian opened the door letting Uncle Maynard enter. I stared at my uncle in disbelief. He smiled back.

Since Monday when Edward Cushing called to tell me that my uncle had died, I had been thinking about him. I planned to write an article in *The Northern Sentinel* about him sharing with all my readers what a wonderful man he had been.

My uncle rounded the table, shook my hand and we embraced. Tears welled up in his eyes and mine. "Todd, it's good to see you. I'm sorry for the charade."

We looked at each other. I was about to ask why when he said, "It's not often one gets to see the future." He paused then solemnly added, "I was diagnosed with inoperable brain cancer two weeks ago. The doctors at Mayo give me two months on the outside. Before I check out I wanted to see how my family would react to my passing."

I looked to Edward Cushing then back at my uncle.

My uncle said, "Edward was following my instructions. He did a very credible job, don't you think?"

"I called my mother on Monday immediately after Edward called. She was terribly upset."

"I called your mother this morning while you were here with Tom and Lucy. I told her about the cancer."

"And," I said.

"She wants me to stop by tomorrow, so we can talk. Yesterday, I stopped at Tobias' nursing home and said goodbye to him. He did not recognize me; it's so sad." Maynard paused then said solemnly, "I wanted to find out when I die whether or not my family would contest my Will. I also wanted to find out if I could count on one of my nephews or my niece to head my foundation."

Maynard looked at his attorney. Edward nodded, "I agree."

I looked from one to the other, "Agree with what?"

"Who will head my foundation," said my uncle. "Todd, I'd like you to head it."

"Me?"

"Isn't it obvious," said my uncle. "Todd, we need to sign some papers today."

"Are you sure?"

"Of course, I'm sure. Ever since you worked in my first dealership, I thought you would one day take over for me. I just wanted to make sure, that's all."

"But I don't have any experience running a foundation."

"Don't worry, if Bill Gates' father can do it, so can you. You have discipline, character and people skills, all of which you will need."

Turning to Edward, my uncle said, "Can you have lunch brought in? Todd and I need to talk about the future."

Another Story

E. S. Oleson

IN THE BED NEXT TO his father's lay a man of similar age, ancient, the features equally pale, the gaze equally vacant.

"Hello," he said to the unfocused eyes, "I'm Emilio's son."

The man turned barely at all in his direction and began to mumble. Ed leaned over to catch the words as they spilled out of the toothless mouth. He strained to hear and eventually made out that the patient was reciting a litany of the cars he had owned in his life. The first was a Ford followed by another Ford. That was followed by others, a Pontiac, a Buick, then a Studebaker. The list went on . . . a Dodge, another Ford. The man became visibly excited by this life's inventory, and from time to time he would back up in his list to correct the year or the model name. With trembling fingers, he counted off their succession until sleep overtook him and the hands dropped to his chest. His eyes closed, and the mouth dropped open, a bit of spittle on the lips.

Ed looked over at his father in his own sleep. He knew his father would regard this man's close company as yet another affliction even though he, too, had his own list of cars. Sleep was his only blessing.

"The debris we leave in our wake and stuff in our pockets," Ed thought. "Damned, worthless lists."

That evening Emilio sat and watched the sun set across the lake. As sunsets went it was a good one, but hard to distinguish from so many others. A mix of cumulus in the distance turning brilliant gold underneath, a smudged mauve over that, still and windless. Another sunset, he thought. He remembered the sun setting in the haze of Delhi, and the abrupt setting into the Patagonia at Bariloche, and how the Caribbean's humid heat between Miami and Havana dissolved the sun and the ocean into one dazzling brilliance.

And then Emilio added that evening's sunset to his own list.

One Bronx Morning

Pat Fogarty

WHEN I WAS A KID, *Leave it to Beaver* was my favorite TV show. The black and white sitcom focused on the life of a young boy whose nickname was Beaver. He and his family resided in an unspecified town somewhere in suburban America. The weekly episodes set in the late 1950s and early 60s totally captured my imagination. But; I never understood why I enjoyed the show so much. The only thing Beaver and I had in common was our age. We were both ten when I started watching the show. As a youngster growing up in a crowded south Bronx neighborhood, I used to dream of being raised in a home like Beaver's. He owned a bike, lived in a nice house and every week his parents gave him a generous allowance. I guess I became a bit envious. Yet deep down, I knew the allowance deal and the cookie cutter house in suburbia was not going to happen in my world.

The earliest memory I have of making a few cents was when my friend Tony Biaggio and I collected empty bottles in vacant city lots for the deposit money. Tony was an only child and the only Italian kid I knew who didn't go to Catholic school. He and his mother lived with her parents in a private house nestled between two five-story apartment buildings. Tony never spoke about his father and I never asked. His Grandmother went to Mass and received Holy Communion every morning, but I never saw his mom or grandfather attend Church.

Although Tony was my age, most people took him to be younger because of his size. He may have been small, but Tony was a tough kid and a real hustler. He knew all the best places to search for empty beer and soda bottles. Most Saturdays, Tony and I would make the rounds scavenging in alleyways and litter-strewn lots for our treasure. I had an old rusty red wagon that I pulled behind me for hauling stuff. We got two cents for the twelve-ounce bottles and a nickel for the quart-sized ones. All the bottles were made of thick glass and the stores would only pay the deposit if they were clean. Tony's grandpa let us use his garden hose to rinse the bottles near the curb in front of his house. That was about as close to Tony's home as anyone ever got. None of the kids on the block were allowed to set foot on the front steps leading to his residence. His grandparents didn't speak English and they preferred not to associate with anyone on the block.

One Saturday morning while Tony and I were washing our collected bottles, Mr. Rosen, who lived on the first floor in the building adjacent to Tony's, stuck his head out of his living room window and said, "How would you guys like to make a quarter each?"

"Wow," I thought, "That's a lot of money."

Candy bars cost a nickel apiece, so I figured I could buy a big Hershey bar every day after school for a whole week. Tony turned off the water to the hose, brushed his black gypsy-like hair away from his eyes, and said, "Yeah, what do we got to do for it?"

The old man pointed to a little red Volkswagen parked across the street and said, "Wash and dry my car and you'll each get a quarter. But, you've got to do a really good job."

Tony turned to me and said, "What do you think? Should we?"

I shrugged my shoulders and said, "Sure, why not?"

The arrangement turned out to be the start of a full-time Saturday business for Tony and me. We were a good team and it wasn't long before some of the other car owners on the street asked us to wash their cars too. I remember making two dollars in one day that spring. I thought it was a fortune and so did my mom. She brought me to a bank on the Grand Concourse near Yankee Stadium and helped me to open my first savings account.

Tony's grandpa would stand on his porch smoking a thin twisted cigar while we used his garden hose. You could tell he was proud of his grandson, and even though he never spoke a word to me, he nodded when he saw me on the street. Getting that little bit of recognition from him made me feel important.

Mr. Rosen and his red Volkswagen became our best customer. We washed his car every week. He could see exactly what we were doing from the living room window of his street-level apartment. I didn't mind him watching us but Tony didn't like it. If Mr. Rosen noticed a spot or some part that we missed, he'd poke his head out the window and holler something like, "I think the driver's door still has a smudge." Or he might say, "Hey guys, how about redoing the hood?"

I didn't mind the criticism. I figured he just wanted his money's worth. Mr. Rosen and his wife were older than my parents and never had children. On weekdays, Mr. Rosen left for work about the same time I left for school, and as soon as he would leave his apartment building, Mrs. Rosen would holler something out the window to him. In my mind I still have a vision of her—half hanging herself out of the living room window in an oversized pink terry cloth robe and yelling, "Stanley, don't you forget my cottage cheese. Do you hear me? Don't you forget the cheese!"

Without slowing his stride, he'd cringe his shoulders, turn his head back towards her and say something like, "Yes Silvia, I won't forget. I promise I won't forget."

Most evenings on his way home from work I would see Mr. Rosen carrying a package or two. If I saw him struggling with a couple of sacks of groceries, I would offer to assist him. If he let me help, I'd usually get a nickel.

I remember a time when he was having trouble trying to manage a grocery bag in one arm and some dry-cleaned garments on wire hangers in his other arm. I asked if I could help and he said no. As he entered his building, the thin plastic covering the garments got caught on the front door and when he tried to free it, the groceries spilled out all over the place. It was a mess and I kind of felt sorry for him.

On Fridays when Mr. Rosen arrived home, he'd change clothes, and then, he and his wife would get in the Volkswagen and drive away.

One morning, after I got to know Mr. Rosen and realized he was a fairly nice man, curiosity got the best of me and when we crossed paths on my way to school,

I said, "Hey Mr. Rosen, where do you and Mrs. Rosen go on Friday nights when you and her get all dressed up?"

He stopped for a moment; put his hand on his chin like he might not want to tell me, and then his face turned into a big smile and he said, "We go out for dinner. Silvia loves Chinese food. She can't get enough of it." Then he gave me a quizzical look and said, "Why do you ask?"

A little disappointed, I looked up at him and said, "Oh, I told Tony you probably went dancing somewhere downtown."

He shook his head and said, "No, we don't dance anymore. Now, get going before you're late for school."

When the school year ended in June, I anticipated that the car washing business would take off—I was wrong. 1960 was a drought year in New York. That meant, during the summer, Tony and I could only wash cars on certain days. I remember the cops driving around the neighborhood making sure that none of the big guys or parents opened fire hydrants for kids to cool off and play in. Tony and I had to adjust our car washing schedule. It was inconceivable to even think that Tony's grandfather would break the law by allowing us to use his garden hose on a forbidden day.

By the middle of July, we started getting plenty of rain, and by the beginning of August, the city reservoirs were almost full. The drought restrictions were lifted, and Tony and I were almost back to our old schedule. But; there was a new problem. We were getting too much rain and most of our customers didn't want us to wash their cars if it was supposed to rain that day or the next.

On Saturday morning, August 13, 1960, I got up early and listened to the weather forecast on my mother's kitchen radio. They were predicting a hot muggy day with temperatures reaching the low 90s. They also mentioned the possibility of some afternoon thunderstorms.

I met Tony at 8 a.m. in front of his grandfather's house. We decided; we had better go knock on Mr. Rosen's door and check with him before we started working on his car. It took a long time for Mr. Rosen to answer, but when he opened the door, he acted as if he was glad to see us. We explained our doubts about washing his car and he said, "Don't worry about the rain. Just go ahead and do a good job."

That was good news for us and we went straight to work washing his little red Volkswagen. We were about halfway finished when a police car came speeding up the wrong way of our one-way street. It stopped right where we were washing Mr. Rosen's Volkswagen. Before the cops had time to get out of their patrol car, another squad car came racing down the street from the other direction with its siren blaring and its cherry red bubble light spinning. For a split second, Tony and I both thought they were after us. I figured, maybe I misunderstood the watering rules. When the police arrived, Tony's grandfather was standing on his front porch with that thin stogie in his mouth. He casually walked down from his porch, looked around, rolled up his hose, and walked back up his steps. The four cops didn't even glance at him. They went straight into Mr. Rosen's building. Within minutes, several unmarked police cars arrived with detectives and the big brass. A crowd of people gathered on the street in front of Mr. Rosen's building. Everyone was trying to figure out what was happening. Two police officers stationed themselves by the front entrance of the apartment building. The cops were polite, but they wouldn't answer any questions. After a while, I noticed a commotion going on in the building's vestibule. We could tell something was up. Just then, two burly detectives emerged with Mr. Rosen wedged between them. He wasn't cuffed. I heard one cop tell another that they were taking Mr. Rosen to the station house in order to get a statement.

When Mr. Rosen saw Tony and me standing by his car, he said to his escorts, "Hold on, I owe these two boys some money for washing my car."

All of a sudden, everyone's eyes were on Tony and me. Mr. Rosen reached into his pocket and pulled out his wallet. He ruffled through the billfold, withdrawing two bills. He handed a one-dollar bill to each of us and said, "You guys deserve this. You do nice work."

As soon as the two beefy detectives and the other patrol cars left with Mr. Rosen, the crowd outside the building disappeared. Tony and I noticed one of the unmarked cars remained parked near a fire hydrant. So, we knew at least a couple of detectives were still in the apartment with Mrs. Rosen. The Venetian blinds in the living room had been lowered, but there was a space on the bottom that didn't touch the windowsill. Tony and I both wanted to peek under the blinds into the living room, but he wasn't tall enough to look in without me giving him a boost, so I said, "I'll look first and if there's anything to see, I'll hoist you up for a look."

Tony said, "You promise?"

I said, "Yeah sure, I promise."

I went to the window, stood on my tippy-toes, and saw Mrs. Rosen sitting motionless in a large stuffed chair with about ten plastic dry-cleaning bags wrapped around her head. Her mouth was wide open, and she looked as if she was about to scream. Tony pulled the back of my shirt and said, "Hurry, there's a police wagon coming down the block."

I backed away from the window and Tony said, "What's in there? What'd you see?"

I felt like puking but managed to say, "Nothing Tony. I didn't see a thing."

By the look he gave me, I knew he could tell I was lying.

The police wagon had the words "County Coroner" stenciled on the doors. As the two attendants were removing the body of Mrs. Rosen from the apartment, Tony heard one of them whisper to the other, "Yeah Scott, can you believe it? The husband swears it's a suicide."

Jibe

Tony Reynolds

HE WAS REASONABLY SURE that his look of concern and husbandly demeanor was convincing. Her doctor was going on about the test they were running, and he hung on the doctor's every word, nodding at this suggestion, pursing his lips at this medical conclusion. But he already knew the outcome or the hoped-for one.

A quarter tablet every three days he was told. The poison would build up doing its damage slowly inexorably. Any greater dose and she would still be dead, but the molecules would pool in her organs and be detected. He had been assured, promised that it would be undetectable, untraceable but more importantly effective. And it seemed it was, he had two tablets left.

The doctor went on. The liver, the kidneys, both were failing. Time was short, treatment options exhausted. Needed to find a cause. But the faithful husband knew there would be no discovery, couldn't be any discovery; ever.

It was late. She was sedated. He told the nurse he needed to go home for a few hours but would return to his wife's bedside that night. Would someone be here to let him into the hospital? Yes, the guard in the emergency lobby would let him in. Gratitude exuded from the obviously exhausted husband.

He showered and pulled on a pair of slacks and a tee-shirt. He had skipped lunch and dinner to make a showing at his wife's bedside; his stomach rumbled a bit. He could grab something out of the fridge before returning his vigil, unless, of course, they called.

He was particular in what he ate: she was not. It showed. She had let herself go, at least to his standards. He was still trim at sixty-seven, an enviable physique, a well-maintained body. She was 'relaxed' she would say.

He thought of the kitchen as two camps in a war zone; his was a Spartan's field, hers was a Bacchus' trough. He opened the refrigerator door and pulled a glass carafe of power drink. He closed the door and gulped down the whole container, almost greedily, eyes closed. When he opened his eyes to watch the last drops slip from its lip to his, he noticed a small note stuck to the bottom.

Her handwriting, 'Sorry dear.' A moment's pause. A cramp, a churning and nausea. His eyes opened wide. He dropped the carafe and spun through to the living room, then to his office at the further end of the house. He yanked open the desk drawer, and an empty bottle rattled around like the tail of a snake. And another note, 'Sorry dear.'

Uncle Harold

S. Resler Nelson

I GUESS LOOKING at it now, my Uncle Harold was a softhearted guy, but he never showed it, except for the last time I saw him. And even then, it was only a glimpse. I had stopped by his farm in Arizona on my way home from college like I had several summers before.

I watched him toil in the hot sun, his face wet with sweat, and his hands cracked and dry as the ground. He looked up and saw me coming his way and drove his tractor on, in the blazing heat and white dust. I admired him when he labored like that, because he knew farming so well, and it was his life.

He stopped in a bit and shut down the rumble of his old Ferguson. He wiped the pouring sweat from his face with his sleeve and leaned back, stretching his hunched shoulders.

I put down my suitcase and looked up at him from under the brim of my baseball cap.

"When did you git here, Joe?"

"Just got off the bus at Hopkin's Corner a while ago and walked here," I said.

"That's quite a ways. You seen Aunt Bess yet?"

"No, I just got here."

"School out for the summer?" he asked and wiped sweat from his eyes with a tattered rag.

"Yeah," I said. "You want some help?"

"Naw, why don't you go and keep Aunt Bess company? Tell her I'll be along for lunch purdy soon."

He always worked alone. He knew how he wanted things done. He started the tractor and I walked towards the house. Across the field, I could see the weather-beaten gray barn and leaning fences. Near the barn was the old, white two-story house. The paint was faded and peeling, and the weeds were high.

I looked back at the golden oats ripening in the sun, and in a barren field Uncle Harold furrowed up the dry earth into clouds of dust.

Aunt Bess saw me coming and waited on the porch. She wiped her hands on her apron and waved. It was good to see her again, as it had been a year. Her small round face smiled.

"We've been expectin' you, Joe. When did you git here?"

"Just a while ago," I said. "Uncle Harold says he's about finished in the field."

"He's workin' too hard, Joe. He's gittin' so thin, and his back bothers him a bunch. He's not young anymore, and with the boys gone, I wish he'd get some help."

"I offered to help him," I said.

"I know, but he don't want no help. He's gonna kill hisself workin'."

"You look good, Aunt Bess."

She stood back and sized me up. "Let me take a look at you, Joe. You're growin' so tall. Is that college teachin' you anythin'?"

"Yeah, I'm going to be a writer."

She frowned and didn't comment, and I followed her into the house. She moved some papers from the table and a cat from the chair, and I sat down. The kitchen was full of fruit and vegetables, canning pots and jars, and dishes not done. She worked as she talked.

"It's been lonesome around here since the boys left."

My two cousins had joined the Army. They told me they wanted no part of farming, and I figured that gnawed at Uncle Harold a lot. But then, I didn't want to work the farm either.

"How's Mary Anne?" I asked.

"Oh, she's fine. Has another boy, so we got three grandkids now."

"That's good. Anything else new?"

"Harold bought a horse."

"A horse?" I said, surprised.

"Uh-huh, traded a couple tons of oats for him last winter." She stopped what she was doing and came to sit near me.

"He's an Appaloosee," she drawled, "but he didn't color out. Harold got him from a rancher near Gilbert. He was thin and had his winter coat, but Harold knew he'd look good in the spring, and he does. He's so shiny now. Real proud and full of hisself."

"I'd like to see him," I said, being fond of horses. There was something about them, and Appaloosas were a fine breed. I remember the old, big-boned plow horses Uncle Harold had when I was a kid. Even they were beautiful to me.

"Harold's colt is so purdy in the morning when we put him out. He trots around with his tail up like a deer and snorts at everythin'. Harold stands and watches him for the longest time before he goes to work."

We strolled out into the sun, and I could see the Ferguson parked in the field and Uncle Harold starting for the house. We walked the worn path to the corral by the barn. Birds lined the water trough and katydids buzzed in the weeds. The air was stifling, and the sun burned high overhead.

The colt was stretched out flat on the ground, his back to us. He was good sized, maybe a two-year-old, a dark bay, muscled and sleek. He didn't stir when he heard us coming.

"He's restin'," Aunt Bess said. "He played hard this mornin'."

She stood at the gate and tossed a pebble that bounced in the dust beside him. The colt didn't move, and she said, "Get up, boy. Come on. I want Joe to see ya."

He still didn't move.

She opened the gate, and I followed her into the corral.

"Well, I don't know. Maybe he's sick," she said. "He's never done this before."

Aunt Bess walked slowly around him, and I stepped where I could see him better, too. His mouth was ajar, and his lips pulled back from his teeth. His eyes were open, staring through a blue film.

"He's dead!" she cried and ran past me through the open gate. "Harold, the colt's dead!"

She came back with Uncle Harold. Tears streamed down her face, and she grasped her apron.

Uncle Harold walked around the colt, and Aunt Bess stood beside me.

"He was fine this mornin'," she said. "I saw him when I went to the garden. He was just standin' there."

Uncle Harold looked long and hard, and I did, too. The colt had a fine-boned face and a long neck. His legs were clean and straight, and his hooves small and trim. There were marks where he'd thrashed on the ground and a disturbed place in the dirt where he'd tossed his head around.

Uncle Harold took off his hat and threw it in the dust. "Damn! Everythin' round here goes bad."

He turned and walked away.

Aunt Bess sobbed, "Why did he die, Joe?"

"Maybe a twisted gut," I said. "I've read where horses die suddenly from that. No good reason for it, either."

"Did we do somethin' wrong?" she asked in a trembling voice.

"No, the colt looks like he's had good care. A horse has a hundred feet of intestines, so as big and powerful as they are, they have a sensitive gut, and things can go wrong. You and Uncle Harold aren't to blame."

I knew a twisted gut, if that's what caused his death, could be aggravated by eating too much sand, and there was plenty of that in the valley. Or he could have had an unexpected bowel obstruction.

Saying something that would lead her or Uncle Harold to blame themselves would only make them feel a whole lot worse than they already did. I could tell they both loved the colt, and whatever happened wasn't from neglect. It was just a freak of nature.

Aunt Bess put her arm around me and then went to the house. I stood by the gate for a long time, listening to Uncle Harold's tractor chugging in a distant field. My uncle wasn't one to talk much or express his feelings, but I knew this colt's death was tearing him apart.

A rendering truck came an hour or so later, as I waited near the horse. Flies swarmed around the bay now, and I tried to shoo them away, but it was no use. Aunt Bess stayed inside, and Uncle Harold's tractor was so far off I couldn't hear it anymore.

The truck driver put a cable around the colt's neck and winched him up the ramp towards the truck bed. The colt inched slowly like he didn't want to go, and his legs hung up a couple of times on the slats.

"Nice colt," the driver said when he was done. "Don't mind picking up an old one or crippled one, but this here's a nice colt."

I tried not to think about it, as the truck rolled through the weeds and out to the dirt road. I watched until it disappeared beyond the cottonwood trees.

My visit was shorter than in summers past, and Uncle Harold died that winter. Aunt Bess moved into town to live with her daughter's family. And the farm was sold in the spring.

The Hike

Toni Denis

"WELCOME TO THE SUNDAY church service," Morty said to the first arrival at the trail, a woman named Penny who had signed up online. She wore a confused look. "This is as close as we get to it, anyway."

The name "Atheist Hiking Club" started as a joke when Ed and Morty first bumped into each other early on a Sunday morning on a Phoenix hiking trail during the winter. They lived in the same neighborhood and had a passing acquaintance.

"Looks like all the atheists are hiking today," Morty said. They laughed.

"I'm more of an agnostic," Ed said. He swiped at a bead of sweat trickling down his nose. "But either way, Sunday is the only day I have to spend out in nature. Saturdays are for errands and my sons."

Morty, a wiry man with Einstein-like white bushy hair and a mustache, nodded sympathetically, even though he'd never had children.

"My schedule is full of volunteer work since I retired, but I always make time for a hike on Sundays."

They hiked together up the mountain, Ed slowing his usual blistering pace so that they could talk along the way. The next Sunday, they met up at 7 in the morning and hiked together again. Soon friends began to join them. After a few months, they decided to try some new trails, and friends of friends came along. Finally, so many people were interested, they began coordinating the hikes via email, then on social media, so when they posted online, they needed a name. They decided to call the group the Atheist Hiking Club. Within three years, more than 100 people were on their list, though no more than a dozen usually joined them on an outing at one time.

Morty had lost his wife to cancer several years earlier, so he was always available for a Sunday hike and enjoyed the company. Ed's wife Calista liked having time to herself for her arts and crafts on Sunday, so he was often available for outings, too.

The two men became good friends, spending an evening a month at dinner together, sometimes with Calista and a friend Morty brought, whether it was Kyle his college-aged renter or a couple he'd known for years from his prior work at a publishing company. He hadn't gone out with anyone since his wife's death five years earlier.

"Would you like us to set you up on a date?" Calista asked over dinner one night when it was just the three of them.

"I couldn't imagine being with anyone other than my dear Miriam," Morty said. "I don't have the heart."

Much of what he and Ed talked about had to do with hiking, from overnight plans to which boots to buy and gear to bring. Arguments broke out over which sock brands were best and what snacks provided the most energy for hiking. While the goal was to travel as light as possible, Morty couldn't resist carrying a large backpack full of snacks and water, a lightweight thin plastic rain slicker, a small fluorescent flashlight, a camelback full of water that he could suck through the rubber tube, an empty water filtration bottle and a first aid kit, among other emergency goodies.

Since he liked to navigate and could use a compass with ease, Morty became the leader of the group. His overfilled backpack made everyone turn to him for any need they had, especially since novices often neglected to carry enough snacks or water. Aside from his walking stick, he always carried a buck knife on his hip, which he'd found useful for digging, cutting briars and as protection. Plus, he liked how it made him feel like Tarzan of the Jungle, he'd joke.

By the end of April, Phoenix mountain hikes were too hot to endure, so Morty and Ed decided to start driving a couple of hours upstate to the mountainous regions of Arizona with altitudes of a mile or more, where the temperatures were cooler and the breezes steady. Far fewer hikers joined them because of the time it took to leave at dawn to get there and then to head back in the afternoon.

Their regulars ranged in age from 20s to 70s. Morty was one of the oldest members, having reached 78 that year. Once a woman in her mid-80s joined them, but she never returned to hike again because she'd had too much trouble with her knees. Morty had descended with her to make sure she made it down the mountain, but it took twice as long as it normally would have.

Today they were hiking a trail called Spruce Mountain, the tallest point in a forested area on the edge of Prescott, one of the earliest Westward settlements in Arizona. The regulars who were there included Colleen, who'd retired as a nurse, a couple in their 30s—Brian and Maisie—who both worked in a prison; Penny, a woman in her 50s who led spiritual retreats for women, Ed and Morty.

"Let's get a move on," Morty said when he counted the attendees. "Almost everyone who RSVP'd is here. We're only missing two men from this area—wouldn't you know, they have the shortest drive."

As he finished speaking, a car pulled into the parking lot. Two gray-haired men, tall and fit looking, got out.

"Is this the Atheist Hiking Club?" the man wearing neon green and purple shorts asked. Everyone replied "Here!" as though it were a roll call. The man on the driver's side bounded out, wearing a red t-shirt and black running shorts and got their hiking sticks from the trunk. Most of the hikers wore camp shorts with pockets, hiking boots, canvas rimmed hats and kerchiefs or headbands to catch the sweat.

Morty stood in front of the group holding a map. "This is a straightforward hike, as long as you stay on the trail and pace yourself," he said. "It's a three-hour climb, accounting for ten-minute breaks each hour. I expect we'll stop for a bite to eat at the top. Everyone stay with the group, follow my lead and you won't have a problem. Any questions?"

"Do you know the trail?" the neon shorts man asked.

"What's your name?" Morty asked him.

"Tom."

"How about your friend?"

"I'm Dallas," the man in the red t-shirt said.

"OK, folks, we've done this trail once before. All I ask is to stay away from mountain lions and bears!" The regulars laughed. "I have copies of the map in case you want to explore and don't want to get totally lost. This trail travels up to a height of 1,700 feet through a pine forest. Mostly the Douglas fir, not spruce. It's a misnomer. At the top is a ranger station used for spotting fires. There are several large boulders on the way, a stream to cross and areas of rock fields. If you have hiking sticks or poles, I suggest that you bring them. It will keep you balanced and possibly prevent any slipping. Any questions?"

"Yeah," said Dallas. "You mentioned bears. Have you seen any?"

Ed chortled when he caught Morty's eye. "Nah. There aren't many bear attacks, but you can't be too careful. We did come across a bobcat once, but he was more afraid of us than we were of him. You need to watch out for mountain lions, though if you stick to the group you should be fine. They like better odds than eight people—maybe just one or two."

Dallas's eyes widened. "What do you do if you see a mountain lion?"

"They're attracted to green and purple shorts," Morty said. "I'd change if I were you."

Dallas began heading toward his car.

"He's kidding!" Ed said. "Just don't run away if you see one, that'll kick in its prey drive."

"You want to get everyone yelling at it and it'll go away," Morty said.

"Oh," Dallas said, rolling his eyes.

"Ed will start the hike, so follow him and I'll bring up the rear." Morty winked at Colleen, who shook her head. The two latecomers walked ahead of them and Morty and Colleen started up the trail.

"You shouldn't tease the newbies so much." Colleen chided Morty as she hiked slightly ahead of him on the narrow trail. "They might decide it's not worth the risk."

"What's the harm?" Morty said. "It's good for them. Gets the heart rate up and prepares them for the climb."

The two were silent as they moved quickly up the trail. The best speed was one in which hikers could talk at the same time they were moving, but Morty liked to stay close to the group, so he quieted down as they rapidly climbed during the first leg of the hike. They stopped when Ed pointed out an owl's nest in a tree.

"Funny, I don't think you and I have ever had a real conversation during a hike," Morty said when they started moving forward again.

Colleen squared her jaw. "That's because you're always too busy chiding everyone and playing the leader. How come you're not in front as per usual?"

"Feeling a bit tired today," Morty said. "I told Ed he needed to lead for a change. I didn't sleep well last night. It's one of those days."

"Your conscience bothering you?" Colleen asked.

"Nope. More like my back, my knees, and my feet. Aging sucks."

"Don't I know it," Colleen said.

"Back until about ten years ago, I rode horses every day. Now I find after the occasional ride that I'm sore for days. It's not fair—I so love to ride.

"That's the trade-off," Morty said. "You get to live, but you don't get to do all the things you love anymore. You have to do what you can at this age. How old were you when you started riding?"

"Six. I thought I was Elizabeth Taylor in 'National Velvet' and that I'd be a champion rider. When I was 13, my mother died, and my father sent me to a convent boarding school for girls. I only got to ride on holidays and school breaks."

"How did you feel about being with the nuns?" Morty asked. They were traversing a switchback trail that climbed higher and higher into the forest.

"I thought it was a raw deal," Colleen said. "I rebelled against a lot of their ways, sneaked out with boys, drank and had sex. I was probably the only Catholic girl in the school who managed to get birth control. But everything came to a head when I slept with a parish priest. They kicked me out, but he stayed on. I always wondered if he had a thing going with the Mother Superior, but I'm sure I'll never know."

"You must have scandalized them."

"You could say that," Colleen's green eyes glittered as she grinned. "My father wanted to lock me up, but he settled for paying for nursing school instead."

"We didn't have nearly as much excitement in the Temple I went to, but we did love seeing the Catholic girls at St. Agnes' School in Flatbush. Those plaid skirts were like a siren call for all the Jewish boys."

Morty pictured the groups of girls in saddle shoes and bobby socks, giggling and walking together with a swivel of their hips. He watched them like a wild species on the African veldt. But he'd only had eyes for Miriam, who had long black hair, dimples and a smile that melted his heart. He had called her his soul mate during their long marriage, so when she died he felt that a big part of him had died. But he'd gone on, as she'd wished, doing what good he could until it was his time to reunite with her.

"Sometimes I wonder whether I could have been a champion," Colleen said. "I have a daughter, Courtney, but she wasn't interested in horses, so I'll never know if she had it in her. Life takes you into the strangest places. She wound up becoming an attorney and works in Manhattan for a big firm. That's my baby, you know? She's a real doer. I miss her so much, but I have to wait for her to come here. She's too busy for me there."

"What happened to your husband?" Morty asked.

"Divorced many years ago. He's somewhere in Duluth, I've been told, on his third marriage."

"That's too bad," Morty said, wondering if it was or wasn't.

"I'd never been so lonely in my life as when I was with him," Colleen said with a bitter smile.

They hiked in silence for the next hour. Morty usually got energized about halfway through the hike, but he had to stop to eat an orange and regain his strength. He sat on a log near the stream. Colleen sat next to him. "Just can't seem to hit my stride today," he confided.

"Yes, well, I'm still waiting to hit mine. This is my fourth hike and I find it just as hard as the first three. Is that ever going to change?"

"Sure," Morty said. "The fifth hike is the charm."

"I don't know why I do it. I could just walk in my neighborhood or play pickleball, but something makes me come back."

"It's the beauty, right?" Morty said. A mule deer appeared several yards away and bent down to drink. He and Colleen watched. The quiet was punctuated by birdcalls and water sounds. A few minutes later, the deer bounded away.

"That does make it worth the trouble," Colleen admitted. "I'll tell you a secret: the first time I did one of these hikes, I was thinking about killing myself. It was on Granite Mountain. I thought when I got to the top, I'd throw myself off. Then at least there'd be people there so my body wouldn't rot in the sun forever. That wasn't long after Courtney left."

Morty was about to pop an orange segment into his mouth, then lowered it. "But you didn't."

"No. I saw an eagle at the top of a tree and I decided that I wasn't ready yet. Still am not. Maybe I won't. The eagle changed my mind and I haven't changed it back."

"Why?"

"I'm not sure. Maybe it was a sign. It seemed to be watching me." She laughed and shook her head. "Then it flew right over me, flew so close I could feel the whoosh of air on my face."

Morty smiled, unsure of how to respond. After he finished his orange, he washed his hands in the creek and they headed up the trail. Pain in his knee made him grunt, but it went away after a few minutes.

As they climbed the mountain, two more hours passed. Morty told her all about Miriam, her paintings, the way they'd dance on weekends until Miriam broke her hip. Then he spoke of how the cancer had killed her. A tear slipped out as he talked about the last days. "She was worried about me the whole time because she knew it would be hard for me. But she'd be proud of how well I've done," he said, sniffing.

"I'm sure she would be." Colleen said. Morty nodded.

"You should find someone who appreciates you, Colleen, it's never too late."

She started to say something flippant but stopped herself. Morty was sincere, so he deserved kindness. "Thanks for thinking that," she told him.

He gave her a tight-lipped smile, grasped her hand and squeezed it as they stared into each other's eyes.

Morty hiked slower than usual, his breathing labored.

"I don't remember it being this hard to reach the top," he panted. They'd fallen behind the group, which up ahead had reached the top of the mountain and disappeared from view.

Colleen, ahead, turned around and waited for him. Suddenly, about 30 feet to the right, across from her, a shadow of a cat sprung out of the brush. In a burst of adrenaline, he ran yelling "NOOOOOO!" toward Colleen, reaching her in time to turn and block the cat's lunge with his backpack. As it fell to the ground with a scream, Morty pulled the buck knife out of its holder on his hip and turned toward the cat, ready to do battle. The mountain lion got up and ran away.

"Jesus, Morty, you stopped it!" Colleen gripped his arm in terror. Morty nodded as he panted. "Let's get away, go to the top," Colleen said, grabbing his hand and pulling him up the trail. The other five hikers had heard the commotion and met them as they reached the summit.

"What happened?" Ed pushed in front.

"Morty fought off a mountain lion!"

Morty tried to speak, but he couldn't catch his breath. He saw the spectacular view of the valley ahead of them, its trees tiny, like the fake pine trees on the model train tracks his father had in the cellar of their Brooklyn brownstone. How odd that the image suddenly came to his mind after 50 years. He wondered what happened to that model train. He pictured his father, younger with dark hair, laughing. When his view spun toward the sky, he admired the deep sapphire blue that spread out above him. Blurry faces hovered over him, but the voices seemed to come from far away, then fade out as his consciousness dimmed.

Ed began CPR, while Colleen punched in 911 on her cell phone.

"C'mon Morty!" Ed yelled as he did chest compressions. Morty's face had no color, his arms lay still, his skin turning a pallid gray.

Several minutes passed, but to Colleen, they seemed like hours. Morty wasn't breathing, he wasn't moving. Finally, Ed stopped. He listened to Morty's chest.

"He's gone," Ed said, tears mingling with beads of sweat running down his face.

As they waited for the paramedics to arrive, Colleen sank down beside Morty's body and took his hand in hers. "Thanks, Morty," she said in a low voice. She thought she heard a whisper in her ear, "You're welcome."

The Chaplain

Pat Fogarty

I ALWAYS TOOK MASS FOR GRANTED. It was something the family did every Sunday morning until dad's heart exploded. After that, mom could hardly get me and my little brother to attend school on a regular basis, never mind getting us to Sunday Mass. God knows she tried but as far as I was concerned, Mass was for sissies. The last time mom got me inside a church, I made such a ruckus talking and teasing my kid brother that Father Puglio stopped his sermon and gave me one of those looks; like he might come down from the pulpit and kick my ass if I didn't shut up. I buttoned my lip but after the way he stared at me, I wouldn't be caught dead in a church. Besides, as a teenager, I had more important things to do. Staying out all night and partying with my buddies Charlie and Dave took center stage.

Mom made excuses for my behavior—poor attendance and bad grades got me an academic diploma from Riverside High. I think half my teachers felt sorry for me, with dad dying during my junior year, and the other half didn't want me back the next year. After graduation, hanging out in Charlie's basement got to be a drag.

NAFTA made sure there weren't any jobs in town; all the factories moved somewhere else in the nineties.

My pal Dave got arrested for breaking into a house. He caught a Judge with a bad temper. Dave got three to five for his first adult offense. I think the judge may have peeked at his juvenile record. About a week after Dave got sentenced my Uncle Joe popped in. I mean out of thin air like some magic genie, there he is in Charlie's basement sitting in Charlie's chair. He starts telling us how things were when he was our age and how bad he had it in Nam and all the bullshit he had to put up with. He goes on and on, I was getting embarrassed. Then he says we should do something with our lives, he tells us to go join the Marines.

I know it sounds crazy but that's exactly what Charlie and I did.

Uncle Joe drove us to the recruiting station and the rest is history. Today I'm a Marine stationed in a little sweatbox of a town called Jordan Junction. After boot camp, Charlie and I got separated. Last I heard, his battalion got hit hard up north near Irbil.

This Jordan Junction place is a smuggling funnel for the bad guys. Al Qaida uses this road to bring all sorts of contraband in from Syria. During the day hours it's not too bad, but at night this place is like Times Square on

New Year's Eve. A huge caravan, three to four hundred Syrian cleared trucks come through every night. Big deal so they got papers that say they were inspected by the Syrian border patrol, they're as bad as their towel head brothers. Every once in a while, a rogue truck will join the caravan. Last week one blew up, killed six Marines at an inspection point and made five others invalids. Me, I'd rather be dead, saw a guy get both legs and some other stuff blown off in Nasiriyah. One minute he's riding in the truck ahead of us, next thing you know he's flying through the air like a scarecrow with no legs. Hit one of those I·E·D's, poor bastard. A medical chopper flew him out, we heard he lived. Damn, if we were going a little faster that could have been me.

That's when I found Jesus, not that he was lost but you know what I mean. I started going to services, made no difference who we had as a field Chaplain. If we had a Baptist Chaplain, I prayed with the Baptist. If we had a Methodist, Lutheran, Mormon, Born Again or whatever; that's who I prayed with. Today I pray when I wake up and I pray when I go to sleep. I pray when I walk over to inspect a truck and when I walk away from one. Yesterday they flew in a Priest to say mass and I couldn't believe my eyes, standing before me in camouflage gear was Father Puglio. He said Mass right in the middle of camp, my entire platoon formed a half circle around him. After mass, he said he wanted to have a little chat with me. I figured I was in for a sermon about being a jerk a few years earlier, but it took several minutes for his words to sink in when he said,

"Charlie is in a better place. His body is en route to Dover Air Force Base."

***

**In the Spring of 2005 while sitting with my wife Susan in a Veterans Hospital waiting room in Arizona, a young Marine who had recently returned from Iraq began telling us about his buddy Charlie and how he and Charlie, two childhood friends, wound up in Iraq. Susan, a Viet Nam era U.S. Army Veteran and a retired nurse from the VA Hospital system listened to every word the young soldier had to say. When the Marine finished telling us about Charlie, I asked him if it would be ok with him if I wrote about him and Charlie.*

This is his story and it's dedicated in memory of his buddy Charlie, and to all the men and women who gave all that there was to give.

Fog In A Trunk

Gretchen Brinks

Letter to Claire Gireaux from inmate Joe Madera
9/4/2004,
County Jail, Santa Cruz, California

Hey Claire,

Wasn't I your Old Reliable all these years? Always there to help with the heavy work in your redwood forest acreage and that big ol' vegetable garden? And remember the 5 a.ms when I picked you up at your sweet-smelling home bakery in the damn fog to deliver your organic muffins to those New-Age-as-hell coffee shops? Good old Joe Madera, slow-moving, big hands and what you call "apple cheeks and clown hair," a guy living in jeans and flannel shirts.

Now I'm stuck in a crotch-grabbing orange jumpsuit.

We're both 32, but you're young and I was born old. You admired the boxes and trunks I built. You loved how I carved their lids "intricately." Making trunks was my labor, carving them my art, getting big bucks for them at craft fairs.

You loved the rare Brazilian wood one I gave you.

Now you hate it, right? Because detectives matched the sawdust on its floor to traces of it on little Manny's body and linked his murder to me.

I wish you didn't know any of this. You accepted me ever since we met at that 1989 Eel River Jerry Garcia concert. You told me, "You're a shy guy and a true original."

A damn loner is more like it; a soul who walked dark roads and deer trails to escape nightmares. All these years, you acted like I was the brother you never had. How could you never see that your good ol' doofus buddy was only a closed trunk of fog?

I'll never again walk your peaceful acres of redwoods or your red cabin filled with batik wall hangings, artsy photos, stained glass, pottery, painted silk, my trunks—all gifts from us craftspeople because we love you and the cabins you let us occupy for free.

You call us family.

I was safe living on your land, away from streets and crowds until you made me sell trunks at craft fairs instead of you doing that for me.

If you hadn't forced me into crowds, some kids would be alive instead of buried in carved trunks in a forest.

I can't stop seeing your wide-eyed, weepy shock when the Sheriffs hustled me in handcuffs to the patrol car on your dirt road. Now I guess you see me on the news. The serial child killer.

Claire, I never hurt those kids. I never put them through what I went through. I committed mercy killings.

Did you really not have a clue? You never asked about my past. "Only when you're ready to tell me," you said. You should've gotten me drunk and stoned, but no. You had to be tactful!

I owe you big time for giving me safe haven before your fatal mistake pushed me back into the world.

I'm going to show you what big old Wooden Joe's been hiding under his invisible lid.

Have you caught on to my fake name yet? Madera: Spanish for wood. I invented it the day I met you and was selling my carved pieces in that parking lot outside the Jerry Garcia show.

Who was Joe Madera before that day? A lot of him is still buried in fog.

My first real memory is a man with a red-brown mustache. He lifted me from a cold concrete floor and held me tight against him. His palm cupped my head and his other arm supported my bottom. "Bring a blanket!" he shouted. "This kid's freezing!" His voice was scratchy like his mustache. Something soft fell over my shoulders and he tucked it around me, soft and then warmed by his gentle arms around it.

I traced the letters on his badge. I started crying.

"You're safe now," he said, but my tears didn't come from fear. I knew he was different and wouldn't hurt me. I cried because I couldn't read his badge and learn his name, and I couldn't tell him mine because I didn't know it anymore.

My whole life until then had gone out of my head. All I had was a remembered image of a woman with a long black braid. She stood at a gas stove, barefooted and wearing a patched dress. She turned toward me and called, "Joselin!" Jose-*leen*, a nickname that means Little Jose.

Little Joe.

Was it me she was calling or one of the other kids I sense in that memory's shadows?

No matter. It's all I know from that life, so I kept the name. Jose. Joselin. Joe.

When my rescuer told me he was Sgt. Gary Mark, the name branded itself onto my brain.

I'll skip the foster home years, one the same as the next, all bad. No surprise: I couldn't make it in those pretty, clean places with rules and bedtimes and nicey-nicey smiles. Didn't know how to act. Threw fits without knowing why. Was baffled when foster parents acted shocked or sad or angry when I play-acted stuff I'd learned in the cold concrete place, though I remembered little of it except in bad dreams.

I ran away, ran away, ran away. At 10, I ran away for good. Social workers and cops couldn't find me anymore or didn't care to. I'll let you fill in the blanks about my life as a San Francisco street kid. You used to be a social worker there, you know how those kids survive. During those years, I didn't think about my lost younger life. I simply hustled and concentrated on staying safe and not getting caught for stealing or for crashing in abandoned houses.

Sometimes the fog inside me cleared, and I'd glimpse the woman with the long braid calling, "Joselin!" And I'd remember Sgt. Gary Mark's scratchy voice and mustache.

I guess I was around 16 when Max Levinsky stepped out of a low-down bar in San Francisco's Tenderloin district. He was an older guy, greasy ponytail, hands beat up and big-knuckled, scuffed work boots. Took one look at me with my hungry eyes and tight pants and said, "Son, you don't need to be selling your damn self. I'll put you to work and pay you and give you a room and no funny stuff."

Yeah, right, I thought; a john is a john. But I climbed into his pickup and damn if he didn't drive way the hell out to a ranch and olive orchard near Fresno! He taught me how to handle horses, work in his orchard and vegetable gardens and do scut-work chores. And damn if he didn't pay me decent money with no "funny business."

And Claire, the best part was, the old coot was a master wood carver. I loved watching him, so he taught me everything he knew.

Max turned me into a hardworking, honest-to-God human being. I felt so good, being busy and doing good work, that my thick, cold fog stayed locked deep down, almost forgotten.

Until the night when I was I think 18 or 19. Max and I were drinking beer and carving. I don't know why, but he lifted his thick eyebrows and growled, "Hey, you really believe you have six damn years of that so-called repressed memory shit?"

I'd confided that to him the first week I lived there. I couldn't believe he'd throw it back at me in such mean, ignorant words. I jumped up screaming like I was possessed, "I don't KNOW."

Then my knife was quivering in the wall next to his head. I ran to the barn and bolted myself inside, so I wouldn't kill him. Loved him. Hated him. Didn't know. He'd been like a father, so why did he turn on me with those mean words? I stayed in the barn for days, seems like, crying and wondering what the hell that fog inside me was hiding but at the same time scared shitless that maybe I'd find out.

Never talked to Max again. When I finally went back to the house, he was dead. I didn't kill him, Claire, honest, unless I caused his massive heart attack.

Did I?

In his will, he left me his land and house and tools. I found a realtor and sold the property. Then I filled the back of Max's battered pickup with his tools, carvings, slabs of wood and blankets, and I peeled out to San Francisco on a quest. "I'm a man now, Max, OK?" Like that, I promised the old guy, my old coot father-type, that I'd figure out how to open the box of fog he'd put me down for having.

It wasn't hard to find Gary Mark. He was still a San Francisco cop, only he'd become a plainclothes detective. No more blue uniform or big badge on his chest.

He almost cried when I told him who I was. He'd never forgotten me or my case. Since I was around 19 then, and acted like I was sane, he decided I was a strong survivor and had the right to know the truth.

What would I be like if he hadn't given it to me? Maybe just the same, I don't know. After all, what he told me already existed under my thick fog.

My memory still hasn't released clear images or the smells or the feel of the men Gary and his team arrested, but when he showed me photos of the abandoned oceanside warehouse where I'd been kept, I understood where my nightmares of cold floors and wet fog came from. All my life I've felt like gray, cold walls surrounded me. Sometimes I'd get flashes of sitting on a cold, gritty floor with a small window up high, framing fog so damp it dripped down the grimy glass. And that bit of memory or bad dream was linked to something bright that blinded me.

When Gary Mark told me my own story, I understood that damn light, all right.

The men confessed that when I was around 3 or 4, they'd bought me from my mother for a handful of hundred-dollar bills. "She was dirt poor, Joe," said Mark. "She and 10 kids lived in a cab-over camper in someone's backyard in Eastside San Jose. She hustled but she was sick. I got that information from your old neighborhood, but she and the kids were gone, and I couldn't find her. Neighbors thought she and the kids left the country."

He figured I was about 6 when he rescued me. "Maybe I shouldn't do this," he said, bringing a worn folder to his desk. "Really think you can handle seeing some rough stuff?"

"I have to know," I growled, and he slid the photos across the desk. They showed me that the warehouse was a small, junky place, not the vast universe of my cement-and-fog nightmares. Movie cameras lay on a table near a film projector aimed at a white wall. At one side was a single bed with a crumpled blanket.

"And these." Mark pulled out photos of a naked, beautiful, small boy: huge brown eyes flecked with green, bowl-cut dark hair streaked with copper, olive-pale skin.

Little Joselin. Little Joe.

Little me.

I felt tears I hadn't known were falling. "I have to know all of it," I said.

"You sure?"

"I have to know what's real and what's dreams."

He brought in creamy coffee for us. Then he ran a video the investigators had compiled from the films they found. "The prosecutor needed this for the trial," Mark explained. "It worked. The jury convicted the bastards and the judge threw the book at them big time."

There stood Little Joe, up close, beautiful body, huge eyes, face blank because he'd sent his mind far away. Then a man entered the scene.

I didn't watch long. I jumped up and slammed my fist into the wall.

"Joe," said Mark, "you know guys like them don't live long in prison. Both those pricks are dead."

Back outside in that 1984 July, confused and raging and crying, I drove hundreds of miles up the California coast, blind to everything but the road and what I'd seen in that video. When I reached the Eel River in Humboldt County, famous for pot and counter-culture, I saw a huge dirt and gravel parking lot. It was crawling with latter-day hippie kids selling jewelry, pottery, beads, food, tie-dye. Giant posters of Jerry Garcia hung against a backdrop of psychedelic colors. It was 100 degrees in the shade, but in the meadow beyond the parking lot, Jerry Garcia was performing.

So, I parked and began selling the carved boxes and beads old Max and I made at the ranch. When I was on my 3rd beer, I got into a conversation with a short young woman named Claire with amazing blue-green eyes, wild Orphan Annie hair and skimpy boobs. With her was her lover, a 19-year-old potter named Jimmy

Medallion, and their friends Stan, a stained-glass artist, and his woman Nell, a weaver.

I had no idea then that you and I and the others would become friends who ebbed and flowed through each other's lives until we ended up years later living and working on our crafts in cabins on your inherited acreage near Santa Cruz.

But Claire, even on that day we met, it was too late.

A few hours before, I was alone in masses of people in tie-dye and selling carved wood while my mind endlessly replayed Gary's video of those men and little Joselin in the cold warehouse.

And then, across the crowded parking lot, I saw Joselin in the flesh.

I swear the kid was my 4-year-old twin: the mirror image of myself in the photos and video. The kid was barefoot in prickly dry weeds while his drugged-out, spotty-skinned mother ignored him, so she could keep selling quesadillas and beer from her rusty van's tailgate. Everyone around her was stoned and partying. No one cared about the hot, thirsty, dirty kid whose feet and ankles were bleeding from prickly weeds and broken glass.

Rage clogged my throat. Fog clouded my eyes.

No one was protecting the boy.

Bastards like the ones who took me would take him too. They'd destroy him, destroy his whole self. They'd leave him with nothing, but a lid nailed over a box of nightmares and fog.

Later, on the posters people put up everywhere, I learned his name was Onilo.

He was the first little Joselin I rescued from becoming me.

No Escape

S. Resler Nelson

SHE DIED INSTANTLY, but I didn't mean to kill her. She fell, and I ran over her. It was an accident, a horrific one. Two others were injured, and I can barely walk. Now I'm in "the pen," scheduled to die. I suppose I'm here because of her death and my own ineptness. That's how we're treated in the end. No one comes to our defense once we're this far down the line.

The facility is packed with others—old and broken, young and unwanted, thin and starving. You name it, we're here. A pretty one with red hair gives me a quick glance. I'd limp over to her, but she looks angry and aggressive.

We mill around in the yard, baking in the hot sun, no food or water to fight over. Not that much oversight either, but there's no escape. A scuffle breaks out, and I avoid it. I'm crippled enough without getting knocked around. A long, jarring trip awaits us, and if I fall I'll be incapacitated. But then why should I care what shape I'm in when they put a bullet in my head?

Enough negatives. I think of my youth and my once promising career as an athlete. They said I was "handsome, a distance runner, highly gifted." I was their rising star, bringing in the big bucks. But the wear and tear on my body took its toll, and as I spiraled down the ranks, so did my favor. Eventually, I was just one of many cranking out measly earnings, another liability.

I'm half asleep, shifting my weight off my bum leg when the main boss saunters in and walks straight towards me. I figure I'll be the first one loaded in the transport. The guy's burly and strong, but there's no satisfaction in his eyes. He leads me out of the enclosure, into the open, and I see freedom. A field stretches before me, and I want to run again, just for the sheer joy of the wind in my face and my body soaring weightlessly over the ground.

Then I see her. She's tall and older, with a kind face. She approaches me, speaks a few words, and gently runs her hand down my aching neck and shoulder and leg. I don't flinch.

"He's got some heat in the leg that needs attention," she says.

"Sure, you want him? We've got younger, healthier ones."

"No, I want *him*. I remember when he was in his prime, and I watched him compete."

She hands the guy cash, and he counts it out.

"He's earned over half a million dollars. Shouldn't that have bought his retirement? Instead, he's slated for Mexico and a slaughterhouse," she scoffs. "He deserves better."

She eyes me again and walks me to her horse trailer. I stumble in without hesitating. As we drive away, I look back at the horses left behind and wish I could take them with me.

Justin

Bruce D. Sparks

I FIRST MET WAYNE at Don's place through my brother Billy. Billy, being a member of the Junior Chamber of Commerce Mounted Posse, owned a horse by the name of Duke that he boarded at Don's place. Duke was a small horse for Billy, who was 6-foot-4 and well over 250 pounds. Duke was a curiosity to me 'cause he only had one testicle. Now why and how this fact came to be known to a 10-year-old boy in the first place is still a mystery to me some 60 years later.

Wayne was a man who had been around horses all his life. His knowledge of horse problems and their cures were always reliable and sound. But he was a drinking man and when on the juice, which happened from time to time, he was mean both to people and to animals.

Wayne owned a horse named Justin, a sorrel gelding with a lot of red in his mane and tail which seemed to be on fire. Justin was the largest horse I had ever seen in my life. He stood tall even for Wayne, who was 6-foot-5. Wayne had to reach up to grab the horn on the saddle to mount him. I was told Justin was a fine roping horse 'cause he was strong and quick from a jump.

The first time I got close to Justin he looked me over real good and wanted me to touch him. He sniffed around my head and neck as I rubbed his nose and stroked his neck. I felt like we would be together till the bitter end, he and I. Funny how those thoughts can come back to haunt you later. I liked Justin and I sensed that he liked me, too.

Don had several head of horses and was always looking for an extra hand to help feed, water, ride, and clean up after them. I would ride my bicycle down to Don's place to work with the horses. I didn't know a thing about these animals, but I was willing to learn and not afraid of hard work.

Wayne and Don worked together in the horse business and made it a practice of meeting often to work the horses and discuss buying and selling. Don, as president of the Yuma Jaycees, Junior Chamber of Commerce, was in charge of several of the other members of the Jaycees' horses that boarded at his place.

Soon I was introduced to an eight-year-old chestnut mare named Zona. I thought, because of being in Arizona, that was a fitting name for her. She was beautiful with a light-colored mane and tail, and very gentle to be around, especially for a kid who knew nothing about horses.

Contrary to popular opinion, a horse will intentionally step on a person and think it's the thing to do. I learned this right away with Zona and soon it became a ritual for her to try to step on me, and for me to avoid getting stepped on. I learned to wash, curry, and brush her, even to clean her hooves. I learned first and foremost how to clean out stalls and change water and feed. Zona was very tolerant of me and I of her. On her, I learned how to sit in a saddle, and how to control a horse and ride. It took months for me to gather this all in and understand the why of it all.

Zona was fun to ride but she had a game she liked to play. When nearing a fence or post of any kind, she would intentionally walk close so as to drag my leg against the object. I thought for some time that she couldn't see well. Once I figured it out, I would just rein her straight into the fence or post. She would give it a wide berth rather than bang her head. She could see just fine. I learned in that short time that horses don't forget things, and they can sense meanness in a person. I was not a mean person with animals, and I didn't know enough about horses to show fear.

Don had a stallion there named Patch who was said to be very mean to everyone--just because he could be. He never seemed to bother me while I was mucking out his stall. Then someone told me that males don't like to stay in a stall with their own droppings, unlike females who will stand in poop all day long and think nothing of it. So, if I didn't keep the stall clean, Patch would kick his droppings out all over the place and act mean. I guess because of my age and the fact that I posed no threat to Patch, he let me do almost anything with him and to him. I could water him down on a hot day, brush him, comb him, clean his hooves, and walk him around.

The one thing Don told me *not* to do is to try and ride him. He said that might be the end of me as a human being if I tried. I hadn't thought much about being a human being prior to that and I took the 'no ride Patch' thing as a challenge. I mean, he was my friend and I did things for him that he seemed to like, right?

One day when I was feeling particularly full of spit and vinegar and bored with the chores I was doing, I walked Patch out to the pasture. While hanging on to the hackamore he wore, I swung myself aboard and expected the worst from him. Patch didn't do a thing, so I gave him some heel. All he did was walk around with me on him like it was nothing. I leaned right, he'd go right. I leaned left, he'd go left. I leaned back, he'd stop.

This was not the excitement I thought I was getting into when I jumped up on his back. I got off and walked around in front of him. He looked at me while shaking his head up and down, with a look that I can only describe as "You are my friend." I had made a connection with an animal and I didn't even know how or why. I did love that horse. From then on wherever I went Patch would follow me. I could ride him anytime I wanted with no problem at all.

Then one day Patch wasn't there anymore. Don had sold him, and my friend was gone. Something I wanted with all my heart, in my short life, was taken away from me and it wasn't even mine to have. I couldn't even say "No, you can't do that." I was devastated over the loss and my two years of working with horses came to a stop. I put Zona and the others out of my mind and moved on with my life without even slowing down. Billy and I talked it over, and he came up with an idea. In Little Britches Rodeo, I would ride horses that I didn't know for eight seconds at a time, and then walk away from them if I could. Rodeo was my way of putting distance between me and the animals I loved.

I think about that black horse and the bond we made more and more these days. Maybe it's my age or maybe it's the need to remember pure, sweet days with a true friend. A friend that knows you for the person you are and responds with all they have. Every boy needs to have a friend that is true. Then he will know for sure those who aren't and give them as little of his time as possible. Don said the sale of the black horse was strictly business and I shouldn't concern myself with it. I have lived my life with people who have said that to me. It's business and not personal, you need to learn that.

Then there was the day that put a lid on my time with horses for the rest of my life. My brother Billy and I went over to see Wayne for some reason or another. I can't even remember now the reason for our visit. When we got to Wayne's place we saw Justin on the passenger side of Wayne's truck, kicking the crap out of the side of the truck with both back legs. I could clearly see a pitchfork sticking out of Justin's right hip. It was in pretty deep and bleeding a lot. The handle had been broken off and only the metal was visible, but it had to have been in his hip about five to six inches and was very painful for him.

Justin was on fire about the deal and had snot flowing out of his mouth and nose, and his back hooves were bleeding from kicking the truck. I could tell this ordeal had been going on for some time as Justin seemed to be getting weaker as he went. Then we heard Wayne yelling from under the truck for help.

Billy told me to try and get Justin away from the truck if I could and he would see about Wayne from the other side. Justin took an interest in us and came for us hell-bent on making us aware of his situation. Billy threw up his hands and started waving his arms and yelling at Justin to stop. But when that horse reared up on his bloody back legs and hooves, he appeared to reach for the sky. I swear he looked 20-feet tall. I know he didn't recognize us. That's when Billy and I ran for cover. I don't know why Justin came my way as I was running, but I knew I had to get on something or under something fast. I went under the rail fence beside the pasture.

Justin stopped at that point and just snorted in my direction. I could see he was bleeding from the mouth pretty badly and had several scrapes and gouges down both sides of his neck and shoulders, which were also bleeding. Justin stood there for what seemed like the longest time just looking at me, the same way he had looked at me the first time I met him. He seemed to say, "Who are you and what do you want?" Billy, by that time, had gotten to Wayne and dragged him out from under the truck. The next thing I knew, Billy was driving Wayne's truck out onto the highway as fast as he could with Wayne in the truck with him. Justin was almost tuckered out from all the excitement and loss of blood, no doubt.

I walked down the fence line toward the house and Justin walked slowly with me on the other side of the fence. I could see where he had gone through the fence, apparently on his way to go after Wayne, and I suspected the pitchfork in his hip was not an accident. I wanted to help him, but I also knew he was hurt. Did your Daddy ever tell you not to get to close to a hurt animal? I sure wasn't about to reach out for Justin right now. Even if I meant him no harm, I wasn't so sure he felt that way about me or anybody.

I worked my way into Wayne's house and called my Dad. He said he'd be there soon as he could. I gave him directions and of course told him about Justin and Wayne. Justin was over by the corral, just standing there breathing hard and bleeding. I kept out of sight from him and waited for Dad to get there. Dad drove into the drive very slowly and came up to the house. I met him outside the front door and showed him where Justin was.

He could see the horse was in serious trouble. So, he went in and phoned a veterinarian he had known for years. It wasn't long 'til the vet got there and looked the situation over. A Sheriff's Deputy was also on the scene as the vet had called them about being there to care for an injured animal without the owner being present. Things were getting complicated, but no help for Justin had been given yet. The Deputy had a Winchester with him and said he'd put the animal down if he got out of control. I didn't want to tell him the war was over, and Justin won. The vet then approached Justin with two syringes full of horse tranquilizer.

Justin seemed played out 'cause he just stood there and let the vet stick him with both needles. Maybe his pain was so great he didn't feel them. Soon he was down, and vet and the deputy pulled the fork out of his hip, with considerable effort I might add. Both rear hooves were split and busted, his shoulders and neck were cut pretty deep, and cuts around his mouth were pretty bad. All in all, Justin had taken a lot of injuries to get at Wayne for what we all knew was pure drunken meanness.

It turns out Wayne had been drinking and, as usual, was feeling mean and hateful. I guess he had gotten into it a bit with Justin over something in the corral. One thing led to another, and Justin got the pitchfork in the hip. Then Wayne got Justin's mouth over his right shoulder. Justin had bitten Wayne deep and hard. Justin's front teeth came down the front of Wayne's chest while Justin's lower teeth went down Wayne's back. The bite was deep and long, tore a lot of muscle and pulled bones out of place, breaking a few.

Wayne had lost a lot of blood by the time Billy got him to the hospital, but they saved him for a short while. Wayne's wounds became septic and within about three days he died. He didn't have much of a liver anyway from hitting the bottle so often and long, so old Justin really did him in.

The County Sheriff by court order went a step further with the situation. The death certificate for Wayne listed the cause of death as injuries and accompanying trauma sustained by an animal attack. Seems when an animal causes the death of a human, no matter what the provocation, the animal is doomed.

Billy and I were at Wayne's place cleaning up after the animals and caring for them as best we could when the Sheriff came to take Justin away. They brought a horse trailer and wanted to load him up and take him on his final ride. They were very clear that they had all the court documents and legal papers with them to do what they were about to do.

Billy and I were amazed that they would even talk about how right they were when that horse had done only what he could do, go after the man that had hurt him. Justin, being all banged up and bruised, was in no condition to fight a normal fight, but he wasn't going without giving them all he had in protest. He knew those men meant to do him harm and he wanted no part of their paper serving, nor any ride anywhere.

As long as I live I will never understand the ending of a life for spite. Wayne died because he was cruel to Justin. Now Justin must die because he defended himself against cruelty. I watched those men shoot Justin and kill him. The bitter end had indeed come, and I was there with him till then.

Just before they shot Justin he walked over to me and looked into my very soul. I touched him and rubbed his nose while he sniffed all around my face. I felt small, I felt hurt, I felt pain, and most of all I felt a kinship from him that only he and I could feel. Billy said it was the strangest thing he had ever seen Justin do.

Some say horses are really smart and act a lot like humans from being around humans for so long. I say they will steal your heart and your dreams about life faster than any woman I have ever known. Broken hearts about women will mend. Broken dreams about horses live forever.

I still remember Justin and his way of dealing with what he was given as his lot in life. Through him, I learned a very valuable lesson about doing the right thing, even at the cost of your life. He had taken all he was going to take from a cruel person, he did what he felt he had to do, yet he remembered me and showed me his gentleness and friendship. Justin will live in my heart forever.

Swordtail

Elizabeth Allbright

ANDY SLUNG THE KAKAI STRAP of her gas mask over her left shoulder, placed her sandals on top of her school books and walked barefoot down the cement walk to Haena Drive. The lei-hua was blooming after the early morning rain on the slope beside the bomb shelter door. As she leaned forward to check for buds, her gas mask swung forward and banged against the tender stalk. The flower shook. Sandy whispered, "It's okay. It's okay."

Sandy looked around the corner toward the Hammaker's yard. Mynahs had set up a scolding chorus. A mynah shot out of a tall avocado tree and dived, pecking her on the head. Sandy felt the top of her head. What have I forgotten? She looked down at her books and shoes. My lunch! She ran up the walk and into her house, slamming the screen door. The lunch box was on the kitchen counter where her mother had put it before she went to work at American Factors in Honolulu that morning. It was the same lunch every day, but Sandy checked to make sure. She felt warm, comfortable anticipation in her stomach. "My favorites," she murmured, thinking of her mom and the homey dessert of oatmeal animal cookies.

On her way down the steep asphalt slope to Atherton Street where she could walk on soft Chinese grass for a while, Sandy thought about her Saturday plans. A fishing expedition to the jungle behind Manoa Valley with Billy. They would ride their bikes to that special place where the strawberry guavas grew, then carry their jars to the stream. She pictured the guppies opening and closing their mouths in the rushing water. Their heads would be pointed in the same direction as they sunned in the shallow, sandy places. But they were almost too easy to catch. Maybe some swordtails would swim into the little new net Daddy had made. Sandy imagined her hand on the coat-hanger-wire handle, dipping deftly in to catch the wily, inch-long fish who wore rainbow shimmers on their silver bodies. To catch one of them would be exciting.

The only interesting thing at school that day was weighing and measuring. Sandy felt good about seeing how much she had gained over the summer vacation. Her old weight when she was nine at the beginning of the year had been sixty-five pounds. Now, a year later in 1944, she weighed seventy-nine pounds. That was a big gain, considering she had been one of the smallest in the class last year. A boy in sixth grade called her fatso when he passed her in the hall that morning. She looked down at her body as she walked home that afternoon to see what he meant. After having Mom and Daddy worry about how thin and small she was for so long, it was really strange to be called fat. The only fat place she could see was in front where the gas mask strap crossed her chest. It hurt there and itched most of the time.

She had been told that the gas masks had been issued to the civilians and military of Oahu when a gas attack by the Japanese became an imminent possibility. The threat of mustard gas scared everybody. The government announced that there was little that could be done to prevent the gas from burning the skin, but it was hoped that the masks would protect the lungs. Sandy listened in horror as her teacher explained that tubs of water would be readied for the children to climb into naked, except for the monster-faced masks, of course. Sandy privately felt that it wouldn't work, besides the school didn't own any tubs. She had decided that being naked in a tub of water with her classmates was worse than getting burned.

She shifted her books to her other hand. Today the class had had a warning from the school nurse to watch out for mosquitos. It seemed funny that a little thing like a mosquito could put its teeny, pointy mouth into your skin to suck your blood, and then leave behind germs to make you sick. Maybe weak, half-sick people were the only ones to get it. "Not me," she said.

Every puddle got a thorough inspection. She zig-zagged home checking for signs of stagnant water. She took a shortcut across a ditch choked with sticky blue plumbago and spied a rusty can filled with rainwater. Two worm-like mosquito larvae wriggled menacingly in it. With a shout, she tipped the can out onto the ground. "There, you boogers! You can't get anybody sick now because you will never grow up!" She stared at the larvae, small as thin rice grains moving feebly on the wet earth.

When she climbed to the top of Haena Drive, Sandy saw Taffy, the next-doors' golden retriever, sniffing at the croton bushes near her front door. Taffy had a habit of growling and chasing her. Sandy had followed her dad's suggestion that she not let out any fear. She kept it locked behind her skin. She advanced steadily toward the dog. By walking briskly past him, she was able to open the front door of her house and slip out of his reach.

"Darn this war," she said to her panda puppet. "I wish I could go swimming. We used to live down near the beach, but ever since Pearl Harbor, we've lived in this house. Now I have to take two buses to get to Waikiki. Besides, I don't like it down there much anymore. So much barbed wire, so many soldiers and sailors. Sometimes they look at me in a funny way. One time I was wearing my bathing suit and stopped walking on the street to fix my sandal strap. A jeep full of men came by. One man holding a camera took my picture. The men all hooted and whistled." She waited to see how the panda took that information. His embroidered mouth seemed to turn down. Sandy sighed. Another hour before either Mom or Daddy would be home. She got a pencil out of her desk drawer and started to do her math homework.

The next day, a piece of cardboard clipped to the spokes of her bike's front wheel played ticking music. It went with the feeling that Sandy always felt when she was starting out on an adventure – a kind of tickling just under her ribs and on the soles of her feet. She pedaled hard up a rise, then coasted down toward Lanihuli Drive where Billy lived. She parked her bike by the front steps of his house and then walked around the house until she was under his bedroom window. "BILLY…BILLY…CAN YOU COME OUT AND PLAY?" Sandy was just gathering breath for another round of calling when Billy himself came alongside wheeling his bike. His bike basket was full of glass jars, just like hers was.

"Here I am. All ready. My mom put some seemoy and some avocado sandwiches in a bag for us to eat while we're fishing." Billy's blond hair stuck up in back. His mom called it a cowlick. On his tan face was a sprinkling of eager freckles. Sandy could tell he was excited because his eyes behind their thick glasses were blinking rapidly. The hated gas mask was left behind under her bed. Sandy laughed. It was going to be a good day. "C'mon, Billy, what are you waiting for?" They pushed off, giggling as the jars clinked in rhythm to their churning feet.

With an asthmatic wheeze, the Woodlawn bus pulled up to its last stop at the end of Manoa Valley. The driver stood to turn his sign around. The thin Marine got out of his seat. "I'll get off here." He was wearing a perfectly pressed regulation uniform with gleaming spit-polished shoes. The bus driver shifted his belly behind the wheel and grinned. "Pupuli," he said. Some of the kamaainas onboard snickered. The Marine patted the gun at his waist. "Going to do some target practice," he said. He knew that respect for his non-regulation gun, for his shiny metal buttons and bars kept their voices friendly, but their fingers made circles in the air next to their ears.

They laughed, wiggling in their seats as if he was in on the joke too. "Pupuli haoli," the bus driver said again. "You're not gonna look so pretty when you walk back to town."

"It's okay," said the Marine. "I can hitch back before black-out." He stepped onto the damp, reddish soil of the jungle that sprawled in ancient disorder at the foot of the mountains. He waited until the bus had turned around, rolling up a rise and out of sight, then he turned to the tangle of trees and vines. He thought about hitching a ride back to the rehab center and shook his head. "Not if I can help it," he said aloud.

The jungle's shade lay only a few feet away, but he hesitated. He needed to clear his mind for what he wanted to do. He went back to last night. He had been resting on a rattan lounge out on the beach front, long after all the other men had gone into the blackout-sealed billet. He knew they would read, play cards or just stare, anticipating the dreams that made them scream in the night. Turning in his hospital issue cot, he'd awakened many times to his own crying. The shrapnel wounds in his legs were healed now. But his brain was hot with memories of the Battle of Midway. Like a radio without a knob to turn it off, it played on and on. Staring up at the paling sky, he had planned to buy a black-market pistol. He knew what he wanted to do on his first pass. Now here he was. The pistol rode on his hip. He fondled it. Dreamily, he pushed aside some branches and entered. He did not notice the small ripe fruit that stained his blouse with its juice.

Something waited for him in the jungle. The scars on his legs felt it. Something in that dark moistness would be a kind of going away present. It would lead him on if his nerve failed.

A metallic blue dragonfly buzzed past his left ear, dipped, then disappeared into a bank of glimmering, dark green shadows. To his left, ginger perfume hung in the air. Like white spiders, the flowers clung to the plants. He turned away toward a sunnier, open area where he could breathe the simpler, wild green smells. Vegetation caressed his ankles, hips, and shoulders. Humming insects lulled the battle noises in his head. Warmth and fecundity saturated the air. He leaned against a tree to rest.

The bus passed Sandy and Billy as they puffed along on their bikes, going in the opposite direction. The driver gave a friendly honk of his horn. Sandy waved absently. Far down the road, she could see the curved space where the guavas grew. She pointed, smiling significantly. Billy nodded. When they arrived, they got off without speaking and pushed their bicycles into the undergrowth.

Some time was spent picking fruit. It went into their mouths and into their lunch bag for later. Eating guavas was an important part of the fishing trip. But there was a peculiar sharp taste to the guava seeds, or maybe it was the skin. Sandy held a guava in the palm of her hand and waited a moment in case there was a message from the Menehune. None came.

Billy pushed on ahead into the leafy thicket bordering the deeper jungle. "I hope we can find the stream in this direction," he said. Sandy hurried to catch up. Once past the thick small bushes, they could walk more freely. Tall trees, koa, poinciana, here and there a banyan, or a sandalwood, trailing lianas, full of quiet birds and whirring insects shaded the stunted undergrowth. The earth was soft and moldy, a comfort to Sandy's sore bare feet already turning orange from the volcanic iron.

"A dragonfly, a huge one!" whispered Billy. "It will lead us to the water." He leaned his bike against a tree and ran after the dragonfly. Sandy propped her bike next to his, picked up a jar, and then followed slowly. It was too hot to run. She wanted to feel the trees, to peer into the shadow. Maybe this would be the day when she would see a Menehune. She wasn't sure she would like one if she did see it. The Hawaiians said they were small men, very strong, with much mana power. They didn't like people to see them. They didn't build fish ponds or gardens anymore. Maybe they had gone to another island.

Her mind was so busy that she wasn't paying attention to where she was going. A sharp kuykui thorn caught on the thick cotton of her shorts. As she twisted around to free herself, she saw a tall man standing in the shadow of an old banyan. He was very still, but his eyes were looking her way.

Sandy wanted to run, but she knew from her experience with Taffy that she must not show fear. She stood holding her jar tightly and looked at him directly. He took a step forward. "Hi," he said in a quivery voice. "What are you doing here?"

Angry now, Sandy said, "I'm looking for fish for my aquarium … my friend and me. This is our jungle. What are *you* doing here? I've never seen a soldier around here before." Then she noticed the black holster at his belt and the bulge of the gun inside it.

"I'm not a soldier. I'm a marine. I'm on leave, just looking around." His smile was a thin line.

Sandy dug her toes into the loam. The gun is all wrong, she thought. She felt her muscles tense. Wary now, she said, "My friend is waiting for me."

The Marine took a few self-conscious steps toward her. He took off his hat and waved it at some gnats buzzing in his face. "I'll just go along … maybe watch you … fish." His hand went down to the holster, resting there.

Sandy's heart was knocking her breath around. She managed, "Okay," then began walking purposefully in the direction that Billy had taken. The Marine was close behind. She could feel the heat of his body. It seemed to reach out to her. She hurried, ducking and scooting around trees, almost crawling through tightly packed vegetation, feeling sleek, like a mongoose. She moved instinctively, knowing that if she were quick enough, agile enough, she could lose the Marine. But she did not dare to run.

The stream appeared in a leafy channel. Billy. Where was he? Her head swung left and right. She almost called his name, but that would tell the Marine too much. Instead, she squatted at the edge of the water, pretending to study it.

Awkwardly, he crouched beside her, looked at her for a moment, and then put his hand on her shoulder. "Don't be afraid," he said. His hand slid around her shoulder, around the side of her halter top, where it rested on a new, round breast. He cupped it gently, smiling dreamily at something behind his eyes.

Scalded by embarrassment, forgetting her fear, she pushed his hand away. "Don't," she said. Angry tears pricked her eyes. "If you are going to be in our jungle, you have to act right."

He blew out a sigh as if he were just waking up. He seemed to think for a long time about what she had just said. He sighed again, "What do you mean *our* jungle? I don't see anybody here but you and me.

Sandy gripped her glass jar. "It belongs to me and Billy … and the Menehune." Suddenly the need to feel a nearness to the ancient Hawaiian nature spirits that lived in the stones and woods pushed her to boldness. "I see them all the time," she said. "There are some, right over there behind the ginger plants, watching everything you do."

"Oh, little girl, the war's made me too old to believe in your Menehune, much as I'd like to," he said.

"They are not just *my* Menehune. They belong to the old Hawaiians. They even dug this streambed," Sandy said loudly so that if there were any listening, they would feel proud of themselves.

Something crashed through the undergrowth downstream. An insect nearby clicked. A breeze whiffled the trees. A few leaves blew into the shallow water at their feet. A startled school of guppies burst into a flower pattern and then regrouped when a lonely, proud swordtail swam into the shallows.

Sandy whispered, "Look." The Marine had a hard time seeing it at first. "There," said Sandy. "Here, you can hold the jar while I try to catch him in the net." He took the jar with both hands. A tickling lightness filled her calves with strength. She pushed herself up in one quick movement, pulling the little wire-handled net from her pocket.

He nodded, rising unsteadily on his long legs. He looked at the child's flushed face, beaded around the hairline with bright drops of sweat. Her face was turned expectantly toward his. The whites of her eyes were so clean that he felt like smiling. There was something he had forgotten. He felt it wither in the blaze of her steady gaze.

"Well?" she said.

"Spunky," he thought. She brandished the net. He said, "Okay, let's get him."

The lightness had gathered in Sandy's throat. She glanced out the corner of her eye at the Marine. He held the jar as if he had forgotten the gun. She swallowed carefully. He stared into the moving water and then pointed to the fish. It was half hidden, now, under a submerged plant. Only its tail was visible, wavering back and forth in the current. "There," he said.

Sandy was poised to dip her net in at the second when the fish would emerge when something pushed its way out of the ginger clump. She jumped, turning anxiously. Billy stumbled out of a thicket of wild ginger, his glasses were perched crookedly on his nose, one bow missing. He wiped his face with his shirt tail. Mud covered one whole side of his body from knee to shoulder.

"Billy, where have you been?" Sandy cried.

He stood there blinking. His chin stuck out. He looked at the marine who kneeled by the stream to fill the jar with water. "I fell in the mud and lost my glasses. Looked for 'em for a long time," he said as his hands made knuckles. "Is he fishing too?"

Yes," said Sandy. "He's helping us."

Billy glared. He marched over to the Marine and started to say something when the Marine yelled, "Quick!"

Sandy gave a mighty scoop with her net, and then deftly released the contents into the jar. The Marine held the jar up to the light. The swordtail glinted in the water, circling curiously. Both Sandy and the Marine whooped and laughed, pointing and saying, "See, see!" to Billy.

"Okay, okay," said Billy. You don't have to get so excited. After all, it's only a fish."

"Only a fish!" Sandy wailed.

"Oh, Billy, you don't know how hard . . . ."The words stopped in her throat.

The Marine saw the exciting light fade from the girl's face, leaving instead an odd greenish expression. She glanced at the gun at his waist, then at the boy. Sudden rage raised the Marine's arm to throw the jar at the boy named Billy, but the noise in his head crashed through the moment, tightening his grip on the jar. He began to sob, backing away from the children, hugging the jar to his chest. "Get out of here," he cried loudly over the din of the battle which roared in his head. Weapons rattled on his left! He saw leaves and branches quivering – a sure sign that Japanese soldiers were surrounding him. His voice rose to a scream. "Go find a hole! Dig in! Hide! It's too dangerous here for you kids. Get out of here, get out!"

They ran. As they crashed through the jungle, branches whipped their faces. Rocks seemed to rise up to bruise their toes. Sandy floundered, feeling that she had never really seen the jungle before. Finally, Billy yelled that he'd found the bikes. Sandy had just gripped her handlebars when she heard the Marine's hoarse shout, a bang and breaking glass.

Breaking In

Dennis Royalty

"PROGRESS IS CRISIS-ORIENTED," a wise man once told me. It's a great saying, so often true. I only wish I'd heard it prior to 1966, when it might have offered some consolation to a fuzzy-faced teen working at Schnaible's Drug Store in Frankfort, Indiana.

Schnaible's was my first job unless you count delivering *The Denver Post* when we lived in Colorado.

I'll get to the crisis part in a minute. First, the setup. This story begins when my parents urged me to earn money for college during my junior year in high school.

Saving at 75 cents an hour was realistic in '66, given I lived at home, there wasn't a whole lot to spend money on, and even if you did, baseball cards were a nickel a pack. My pal, Andy Mitchell, already was a stock boy at Schnaible's—so there was added incentive to work there.

"Stockboy" actually was "do-anything-boy" on nights and weekends. We added price tags to everything, from aspirin to shoe polish, and carefully positioned new stock behind the old as we shelved items in neat little rows. But the job also required everything from bagging for the cashier to working the register when Marguerite took a break, to cleaning the stockroom and the bathrooms, and--very important to owner/pharmacist Fred Schnaible—helping customers with a smile.

Smile I did, but I also tilted toward harmless smart-alecky at times. This behavior was limited, usually, to shoppers I knew as they entered Schnaible's with a "help me find it" expression.

"Looking for Alka-Seltzer?" I'd say.

"See that Coke machine back in the corner?

"It's nowhere near there." (Fear not: I quickly steered folks to their quest. No harm was done, and a little boredom lifted for me.)

Excitement came to Schnaible's every six weeks or so with the arrival of the Kiefer-Stewart truck, bringing sales merchandise ahead of our ad in the *Frankfort Morning Times*.

That's when Andy and I had to hustle. We needed to unpack what the truck brought to the stockroom, then get it marked and displayed before the ad hit *The Times*.

I'll never forget Bon Ami cleanser, priced at 9 cents a can. Kiefer-Stewart unloaded what seemed like hundreds of the round containers, each invariably coated in a flour-like cleanser. We got them priced and shelved on time but wore Bon-Ami powder for the rest of the shift.

Andy and I stacked Kiefer-Stewart boxes floor-to-ceiling in the stockroom. One day, we giddily yanked open a large container marked "Superballs" that had been precariously stacked atop other boxes, within reach but at least 8 feet up.

A cascade of bouncy orbs ensued in all directions. Dozens hopped about as if they were alive, making such a commotion that Mr. Schnaible abandoned his post to check out the noise.

This was one of the rare times when Fred Schnaible looked over his bifocals at us, red-faced and exasperated. The rubbery balls not only caromed off his legs but, worse, some bounced beyond and into the store.

Who knew Superballs didn't come in individual packaging?

The Superball episode aside, Mr. Schnaible was tolerant, forgiving, and kind. He and another good-natured pharmacist, Dave Decker, not only managed the pharmacy but ran the entire store, dividing a seven-day workweek. In their eyes, I was a conscientious worker, arriving on time, a self-starter. Schnaible's seemed a perfect fit for me.

Until, that is, pharmacist Steve Decker arrived—Dave's younger brother.

Mr. Schnaible had another store in Lafayette to look after, so needed more help. Steve was tall (maybe 6-3) and thin, with a drill sergeant-looking crew cut and personality to match. The fact that the pharmacy area (off-limits to anyone but pharmacists) was built a couple of stairs higher than the rest of the store made him seem all the more intimidating.

The honeymoon was over for Andy and me. Me, especially.

"DEN-NIS." "Oh, DEN-NIS!" Steve's voice carried to the supermarket next door and the parking lot beyond.

A task hadn't been done to his satisfaction. I was in the crosshairs as I hurried to his pharmacy perch.

How long had I been working here? What else did I need to have explained to me? On and on he went. Before Steve, coming to work was pleasant. His demanding style changed that. And it kept me on edge.

I can't blame what happened next on Steve Decker. But in my defense, I was doing a lot of looking over my shoulder when he ran the store, my confidence wavering.

And so, it was when I confronted the dreaded routine of refilling distilled water bottles.

Frankfort was well known for its hard water, so distilled water sales were high. Schnaible's carried one-gallon glass bottles that were returned after use. It fell to Andy and me to peel off the old labels, affix new ones, and refill the bottles.

Refilling them meant pouring water into each bottle from sizable 5-gallon glass jugs.

At this point, I must confess that arm strength has never been, well, a strength for me. When a 5-gallon glass jug was full, it was all I could do to hoist it in the air, aim it at a glass funnel placed in the mouth of an empty bottle on the floor, and pour in a gallon's worth.

Once the empty was full, I'd remove the funnel, cap the newly-filled bottle, and repeat the same hefting chore until enough one-gallon distilled water bottles were ready to restock the shelves.

Along came a Saturday morning where things weren't going well. Andy was off, and I had much to do. Leaving the distilled water refilling to his next shift wasn't an option. Naturally, when it came time to refill empties, the 5-gallon jug was completely full. This maximized the degree-of-difficulty for me.

I placed the glass funnel into the mouth of an empty and lifted the large jug, staggering under its weight. Distilled water surged forth, slopping beyond the funnel. Suddenly I was off-balance, grappling with a-now-slippery 5-gallon jug.

Out of control and out of my hands it went, like a dirigible crashing to earth. Only, in this case, the massive jug slammed into the glass funnel and glass bottle below, smashing them to pieces.

A resounding crash brought pounding footsteps from the pharmacy section, just outside the stockroom.

Steve Decker's eyes caught me at my worst, fumbling to retrieve hunks of glass but skidding on a flooded floor.

"IDIOT! IMBECILE!"

"Clean up this mess right away! Get the rest of those bottles filled!"

But then Steve realized there could be no more distilled bottles filled this day, or any day in the near future. That's because our glass funnel was in shards on the floor. Schnaible's had no other suitable funnel for the task.

"Now you've done it," he thundered. Only an influx of customers at the pharmacy counter halted the onslaught. And prevented Steve Decker from seeing tears in my eyes.

It didn't take Mom and Dad long to realize something was up when I got home. After some blubbering and consoling, Dad produced hope.

"I think we've got similar funnels at work, let me check."

Back he came from the National Seal plant with not one but two funnels, a glass one, similar to what I'd broken, and a same-size plastic funnel. A godsend!

I couldn't wait to get back to the store. Steve was alone in the pharmacy area when I rushed up to him.

"Look what I've got," I said meekly, pointing to a paper bag I carried.

"What now?" he said, descending the stairs.

Triumphantly, I reached into the bag. I would show him! Inside, I had sleeved the funnels. I grabbed one and whisked them out, triumphantly.

"Here you go," I beamed.

But I was gripping only the top edge of the plastic funnel.

From beneath it slipped the glass funnel.

Which plunged to the tile floor, end over end.

And smashed into pieces.

Teeny, tiny pieces. Glass everywhere.

I froze.

Steve did too, eyes bulging.

Finally, I managed a gasp, incredulous. And awaited Mount Vesuvius to explode.

He did. But in laughter.

Loud, belly-grabbing, raucous laughter. Recognition of the absurdity-of-it-all kind of laughter.

And then he touched my shoulder--not to send me reeling, but in a caring way

Steve Decker wasn't laughing at me, he said.

Things happen.

Everything will be OK.

"But how about getting a broom and a dustpan, to clean this up?"

Things were never the same between us after that. Instead, they got better, much better.

We still had a plastic funnel. He even thanked me for bringing it in.

So, from the apparent worst, progress. Crisis-oriented progress, to be sure.

But a good kind of progress, as progress so often is.

Memory Loss: Aid to Physical Fitness

Shirley Willis

EVER NOTICE, WHILE ELDERING WITH GRACE that you've acquired, along with stray nose hairs and fragile bones, a bit of difficulty with remembering where you put that, um, comb? And the cute flowered sneakers? And the pink fuzzy sweater? Or what you were going to do with them? That happens to all of us, right? So, this morning, rather than pulling a frowny face, I ran the reel of ageless pep talks about turning challenges into strengths—while still in bed, of course. That put me back to sleep faster than a fistful of Ambien.

Seventeen minutes later, I awoke all motivated and self-directed. While stretching I plotted how I'd repurpose my misfiring memory as the catalyst for calorie burning. Today, if I lost something, I'd slap on my Fitbit and rack up the steps. It went like this.

I searched the bedside table for my eyeglasses and knocked over a stack of books. I rearranged the books, searched under the bed for the glasses and found my long-lost slippers, two mismatched socks, and enough dust to form half a person—a hundred calories, I calculated. I put on the slippers and stumbled out of the bedroom to locate the dust mop. On my way, I stopped by the coffee pot for a wake-up jolt and promptly spilled coffee on my newly retrieved slippers because I can't see as far as my feet without glasses.

I visualized. "If I were a pair of glasses, where would I be?" This works every time, right? Not really.

One of those funky light-bulb moments struck. My glasses must be on the couch where I nearly wet my pants—another challenge—watching Betty White in reruns of "Hot in Cleveland" last night. Man, what I'd give to have her writers directing my script.

I straggled into the great room. Searched the couch. Searched under the couch. Located the remaining half of dust to create a person. Remembered when creating a person was way more fun and burned oodles more calories. Remembered the dust mop for under the bed. And now the couch. Headed to the laundry room on the opposite side of the house. Got halfway there and remembered my glasses. Went back to the couch. Searched some more. Gave up. Remembered the coffee. Headed back to the kitchen counter. Groped for the cup. Slipped on spill. Checked for broken bones. Thought, "This is how it all ends." Racked up another hundred calories. Remembered my glasses again.

A mental image blinked, showing glasses perched on the bathroom counter where I was reading a prescription bottle before bed last night. Was that only last night? I headed back through the bedroom and tripped on the dust from my earlier—I think it was earlier today—under-bed search. Checked again for broken bones. Not yet. Shook half person off my pajamas. Sneezed. Sneezed two more times. Blessed myself. At least another hundred calories. Headed to the bathroom for my glasses—more calories.

Eureka. Glasses found. I slammed them on my face, adjusted them while checking the mirror and decided it must be a fake mirror. Nobody looks like that, not even in the morning. Back in the kitchen, I rewarded myself with a double-chocolate, frosted, applesauce and raisin muffin for all the calories I'd burned.

Total Benefits:

Walking, bending, reaching, sneezing and growling. Chewing, well more like sucking. I calculated the calories adding brain activity which also burns major calories. I checked the clock. I'd only been up for seven minutes and burned three hundred calories. Well, maybe it was three hundred calories. My math was never that good. I traded the coffee for chocolate milk with a morning scoop of ice cream and forgot the calories. Chocolate fix on board, I had enough strength to find my Fitbit. Tomorrow, I'd tackle addition and subtraction. Now. Just where was the Fitbit? And the dust mop. And . . .

Did We Remember to Buy the Rings?

Steve Healey

I WAS NEVER what you would call a handyman. At a relatively young age, I experienced an epiphany. I realized I was the reason God had created plumbers, painters, and electricians. If the screwdriver or wrench wasn't working, I would grab my favorite tool the hammer and make fast work of whatever the project was. If there were parts left after I assembled something, I would put them away in case I ever found out what they were for. If the object I built didn't teeter or fall apart right away, then, in my mind, there was no need to worry about the leftover parts. Two or three years later I would come across the parts and still have no idea what they were for. Of course, I still couldn't throw them away, you never knew when you might need them in case something did fall apart. So, I would add them to an ever-growing stash of unidentifiable leftover parts.

Normally the most valuable and expensive player in my lineup of admired handy people was the auto mechanic. He was indispensable. If a washing machine broke, there was always the laundromat. If the wiring needed to be replaced in the house, it could wait as long as the house didn't burn down. But when the car wasn't running? That was a major catastrophe requiring immediate addressing. Even though a visit to the mechanic always seemed like highway robbery, whatever was wrong with a car had to be fixed. Period. No matter what the cost.

Though my step-dad was pretty handy with tools, for the most part, he didn't mess with cars and auto shop was not an elective in my high school. So I learned nothing about cars except how to drive them. Auto mechanics continued to be wizards in my book.

My lack of mechanical knowledge came to light in a big way when I was in the Army. While in Viet Nam, I was assigned to perform preventive maintenance on our radio repair shop's truck. A much better preventive maintenance plan would have been to keep me from performing preventive maintenance on *any* truck. I was assigned to do a minor maintenance that included an oil change. I thought I'd done an ok job. I replaced the oil filter and checked the tires to make sure the pressures were correct. The lights and communications radio were working fine, all connections were made, and everything was in good working order. I drained the old oil, replaced the drain plug and put the new oil in. Everything on the checklist was checked and I was headed back to the radio shop feeling good that I had actually done an oil change and light maintenance on a small truck for the first time.

As I drove the truck back from the motor pool, it suddenly stopped running. The engine refused to turn over when I tried to restart it. After the truck was towed and checked out, it was determined that I had refilled the engine with a solvent instead of oil. There were barrels of each sitting right next to each other in the motor pool. I must have grabbed the wrong hose when I went to refill the engine. My minor preventive maintenance had turned into a major engine replacement. For the rest of my army career, I was never again assigned preventive maintenance on any vehicle.

Five years later, I'm back in civilian life and no more knowledgeable about auto repairs. I had a '68 VW that developed a severe oil leak. It was bad enough that it could have seriously damaged the engine. Young and relatively poor at the time, I had no idea how I could find the money to fix the engine. I had a good friend at the time named Wayne who was an active duty Air Force pilot and had actually taken auto shop in high school. He said he and I could rebuild the engine and save me a lot of money. Who was I to disagree? The price was right.

"VW motors are like glorified lawnmower engines. There's nothing to them," Wayne assured me. "We'll break that puppy down and rebuild it in no time. It'll run better than new when we're done with it."

"Neither of us has a garage. Where do you plan to do this?" was my question.

"On the dining room floor in my apartment, of course. The engine is small and light enough that we can pull it, put it on a dolly and wheel it into the apartment." And that's just what we did.

So, after buying a copy of *HOW TO KEEP YOUR VOLKSWAGEN ALIVE—A MANUAL OF STEP BY STEP PROCEDURES FOR THE COMPLETE IDIOT*—which I still own today, we proceeded with the resurrection of my car. According to the manual, there was actually a cassette recording available allowing you to compare what a normal VW engine sounds like versus engines with various problems. Even though it sold for only $6.50, Wayne believed we didn't need it.

Wayne flew C-141's out of McGuire Air Force base and was gone much of the time. During his trips, my deconstructed engine sat on his dining room floor, staining the carpet through the newspapers and blankets we had put down. When he returned from his trips, our "engine sessions" would start well enough. But then, as the partying began, we would veer off the intended flight path and end up crash landing after a couple six packs of beer and whatever else we happened to be indulging in at the time. As a result, it took almost two months to finish rebuilding the engine. Of course, other interruptions like realizing on a Sunday evening you forgot to buy the new rings, having to have the bearings pressed onto the crankshaft three times after bending them out of shape twice, and purchasing the wrong gaskets a couple times also tended to slow things down and give rise to the "Oh well. The hell with it. Let's just party" attitude.

Slowly, but surely, the engine went back together and finally, the day came to reinstall it. Amazingly, it went back in with a minimum of problems. It matched up perfectly with the motor mounts and everything reattached easily. We had installed new wiring, spark plugs, filters, even a new battery. We added the oil and checked and double checked to make sure we had done everything correctly. It took a bit of coaxing, but the engine finally fired up after 4 or 5 tries. It sounded so sweet that I thought about recording the sound on a cassette, so I could send it to the manual's author. I wanted him to know he had nothing on Wayne and me. I drove the car home the five miles from Wayne's place to mine.

The next day my friend, Donna, came over to my place. All proud and excited about rebuilding my car, I suggested that we go for a ride. I wanted her to hear how good the rebuilt engine sounded. Driving down a street just a few miles from home, I lost power. The VW just conked out. All of a sudden, I "flashed back," thought about the truck in Viet Nam and had a bad feeling.

I coasted to the curb in front of a house where a man was watering his lawn. I got out, walked around to the back of the car where VW engines were located and lifted the hood. The engine was on fire.

"Donna, you may want to get out of the car," I announced. "It's on fire." Needless to say, Donna, who would eventually become my wife in spite of that day's heated activities, was not nearly as calm about the situation as I seemed.

Turning to the man watering his lawn, who by that time had a rather panicked look on his face, I asked for help. He said sure. He responded by running into his house, coming back out with his keys, pulling his car which was in his driveway into his garage and disappearing back into his house. Evidently, he finally called for help because a few minutes later a police car came racing down the street, lights flashing and sirens wailing. The officer jumped out, opened his trunk, pulled out a fire extinguisher and instantly put the fire out. The new wiring, belts and plugs and all the work we had put in was just a pile of melted plastic, burnt rubber, and nasty smelling smoke.

About 10 minutes later, the local volunteer fire department finally arrived on the scene. One of the firemen, dejected because he missed the fire, grabbed a pair of bolt cutters and proceeded to sever the battery cable that ran through the firewall and into the battery compartment under the back seat. Even more major damage.

"You can never be too sure," was the fireman's self-satisfied justification.

Eventually, I did find out what caused the fire. There was a tiny hose between the carburetor and the fuel pump that we had forgotten to replace when we put the engine back together. It was old and frayed. It had worked itself loose and started leaking gasoline all over the engine which then caught fire. For the sake of a two-inch, fifty cent hose, the greatest mechanical accomplishment of my life had crashed and burned.

That day I learned to live by the axiom that it's cheaper to call someone who knows what they're doing right away instead of having to call them after you've totally screwed things up.

I don't refurbish bathrooms. I don't build birdhouses or remodel kitchens. I don't even put oil in my car. I open the hood, look around, instantly get lost and close the hood again. The only thing I know for sure is where to put the window washer fluid. After that old VW motor, I don't mess with anything under any hood anymore.

So, thank you, God. Thank you for making all those carpenters, computer techs, and shoemakers. For the tailors, the bricklayers, and the refrigerator repairmen, who were the original pioneers of baggy pants. And most especially, for the auto mechanics.

And thank you to Wayne, wherever you are, for teaching me the value of earning enough money to be able to pay other people to fix my things right the first time.

Dad Gets Buzzed

Tom Spirito

During the Second World War, my Father served in the Eighth Air Force and was based for a time in the London area of England. He experienced a period known as the V-Blitz. During the summer of 1944, Germany began raining down upon Britain a new terror weapon. The Nazi's called it Vengeance One. The Allies called it the Buzz Bomb. This was the granddaddy of the cruise missile, carrying a one-ton explosive warhead, but with a guidance system so primitive it needed to be aimed at a target the size of a city. London became one big bullseye.

Between the more traditional night aircraft raids and this new menace, my Dad was getting a bit weary. Night after night his sleep was interrupted by the air raid sirens warning of the approaching enemy. These alerts required all the men in his Quonset hut, a sort of mini barn shaped building with a roof of metal, to leave the "comfort" of their improvised abode and head for the protection of a slit trench outside.

After many of these uneventful nightly interruptions, Dad decided it wasn't worth the effort to get out of bed. So, the next night, as the sirens began to wail, Dad decided to pull the covers over his head and stay in bed. It wasn't long before he heard a disturbing sound. It was getting louder, closer, and sounded like a pulsing BUZZ. He next became aware of a noticeable vibration that began to shake his temporary home. The hut started swaying along with his cot. Dad jumped from and scrambled under his cot. The Buzz Bomb seemed to pass directly overhead and exploded a half-mile away.

Dad always called his branch of the service The Air Corps. He would proudly sing and knew all the words to 'The Army Air Corps' song. He'd always loved the line "give 'em the gun" and would point both hands like they were guns and make a machine gun rat-ta-tat kind of sound effect.....what a character. He also emphasized the lines "they live in fame, go down in flames" and would make a motion with one hand of a plane going down. Not that he was ever in much danger of going 'down in flames,' but I think that night under the cot was as close as he wanted to come.

Dad did admit that after that night, when the sirens sounded their mournful warning, he was the first man out of his bed and into the slit trench. "Fool me once" he would say, as he pointed skyward with a twirling index finger, and smile a crooked smile, with his eyes wide open.

The River of Life

Bruce Paul

Kayaking: I like the word. Unlike Tolkien's reputed fondness for *cellar door*—not because of the intrinsic beauty—but nonetheless, I like it.

Despite my experience.

It was autumn. Linda and I were on vacation in the Ozarks, in the remote woods of Missouri, looking forward to a week of relaxation. We rented a treehouse overlooking the river—literally overlooking the North Fork of the White River. From our deck, we could look down into water as clear as snowmelt in the Rockies. The river is spring-fed (Rainbow Spring alone pumps almost 140 million gallons a day into the flow) and provides some of the best trout fishing in the country.

And there is the whitewater.

I am not a fisherman, nor had I ever been kayaking.

Occasionally, a group of two or three kayaks would float by our treehouse—people merrily making their way toward Arkansas. I'm sure beer was involved. They would wave to us, and we would wave to them.

Early in our stay, I asked the proprietor of this little retreat community how he came to have the property, and he explained: After his father drowned in the river, he went to live in Arizona with his mother. Eventually, by inheritance, the land was his, and he began building treehouses and renting kayaks.

Drowned in the river?

On the third day, we decided to try kayaking ourselves.

The arrangements were simple enough: In the morning, be at the office at the appointed hour. A van would take us north to the drop-off point. From there we would float downstream at our leisure, back to our community in the woods.

In the shop, at the office, I saw the display of water shoes, but it meant nothing to me. I had never heard of water shoes. I also noted several signs informing me that—by law—the proprietor who rented equipment to me had no responsibility for my death.

OK. Fair enough.

In sight from the office, rapids roiled the river. We had a few questions. Clearly, on our return, we would have to navigate through this turbulence.

Paul, one of the staff, happily instructed us. "See that little channel on this side of that big rock? That's where you want to go."

"OK."

Sensing my concern, he added, "People do it all the time."

"And there are more of these along the way?"

"Oh, yeah. But it's mostly just an easy float."

"OK."

"Don't worry. If anything happens, just stand up. The river is shallow. Just stand up."

It wasn't the depth that concerned me. It was the rocks.

We headed north in the van.

The owner and another man, a guest at the retreat, sat in the front. Linda and I, and the other man's wife, were in the back. The road was unpaved for miles, until we got to the highway. The van bounced and rattled, and it was hard to hear any conversation, but I could make out some of what the owner was saying. Clearly a religious man, he was explaining how he wanted to provide opportunities for ex-convicts upon their release from prison. I think he was planning to set up a repair shop of some kind. The men could live on the property somewhere, work in the shop, and eventually return to the larger world with some skills and a new view of life. This was of some interest to me, because many years ago, I was a counselor in a maximum-security prison, and I wasn't sure about ex-cons living at a vacation retreat.

At the drop-off point, the sand and gravel ran smoothly down to a still cove. Easily, we were in the water, ready to go. We had rented sit-on-top kayaks—the kind you climb onto, not into (more like flip-flops than moccasins). Linda, being 80 pounds lighter than I am, took the cooler. I had only what I was wearing: swim trunks, a T-shirt, flip-flops, sunglasses, and a baseball cap. In my pockets, I had a camera, some cash, and a key to our treehouse.

Surprisingly cold, the river was as clear as vodka.

Photos were taken.

The adventure began.

Sometimes paddling, and sometimes just floating, we went with the flow.

Learning to steer was fun. Occasionally, we just floated backward, enjoying the view of where we had been. We would pass one another, taking turns being the lead. We took photos of everything: each other, a rock formation, an eagle's nest, the eagle majestically soaring . . . . Sometimes, in places where the river barely seemed to flow, we would paddle back upstream to get a second look. At other times, the flow quickened, and we would just float. Every now and then, we pulled alongside each other and passed the camera.

Eventually, we came to our first rapids.

No problem.

There is nothing like the first time—except maybe the last.

Now we were cruising. Occasionally, amid the rapids, one of us would hit a gravel bar, but it was always easy enough to push off with a paddle and return to the flow. I had fewer incidents than Linda, and I was becoming quite confident.

In time, at a sharp bend in the river, we decided to stop for lunch. We dragged our kayaks onto the shore, took the cooler to a shaded spot, found some rocks to sit on, and enjoyed a sandwich and a beer.

Then, it was time to move on. I removed my T-shirt. Linda took it and stowed it with the cooler. She passed the camera back to me, and I put it in my pocket. We were on our way.

I was in the lead as we floated lazily downstream. The sunlight was warm on my shoulders, and I was relaxed.

Rapids ahead.

The foam was to the right. There appeared to be a smooth course straight ahead. Here we go!

The next thing I knew, I was grounded on a gravel bar.

Not a problem. I had been here before.

But try as I might, I couldn't push off. I tried rocking *and* pushing with the paddle. Nothing. I tried to push off with my foot, but the rocks were slippery and sharp, not what I expected. This was not going to work.

I found my flip-flops and put them on.

I climbed off the kayak, so it would lift.

Immediately, it was ripped from my grip—taken by the current—and I was knocked down. My flip-flops were gone.

Stand up.

I tried to stand, but the current knocked me down and dashed me into the rocks.

Again, I struggled to stand, but the river was mighty. Whenever I tried to gain my footing, the current overwhelmed me. My feet hammered the rocks.

Tried again. Knocked down. For a moment, it was comic. Then, it became cosmic: Accept the pain, and try again. Only to be overwhelmed, swept away, and bashed.

A gallon of water weighs 8.3 pounds. A rushing river is incomprehensible.

By now, I had no idea where Linda was. I didn't know if she had passed me. Maybe she was still behind me, floating backward, admiring the scenery. Or maybe she was horrified, watching me crash through the rocks. Not that it made any difference. There was nothing she could do.

I am no stranger to chaos and drama in the water. In college, in the summers, I was a lifeguard. We saved people almost daily. There was even a time back then, in the flooding of early spring, when I took a life raft over a dam—just for the adventure.

Fifty years ago.

Now, on the North Fork of the White River, I was thinking: Flow with the current. Work toward the bank. As I was battered against the rocks.

I grabbed for a tree limb that reached out over the water.

But I was swept away.

I grabbed for another limb and was swept away again.

And again.

I clearly remember thinking: THIS IS SERIOUS.

Suddenly, miraculously, the paddle I was gripping in my left hand caught in something—limbs or roots—I don't know—and I slammed into the turnpike it made. The current pounded me against it.

Now, I was able to cling to a limb.

And I was not about to let go.

With my left hand, I was trying to protect my ribs from beating against the paddle. With my right arm, I was clinging to the tree.

Never in my life had I called for help.

Although futile, this was not completely foolish. There were summer homes and cabins nearby.

"Help!"

Was this like a car alarm in the city? Or maybe everyone was inside on the Internet?

"Help!"

The current ripped off my trunks.

Now I'm naked, clinging to a tree, banging against a paddle handle, calling for help.

Time slowed, and my thoughts raced, but I had no solution to my predicament.

Out of nowhere, to the rescue, Linda arrived.

Thank God.

She maneuvered her kayak near me, and I managed to pull myself across the bow—my cold white cheeks rising from the water.

Linda shouted, "Get off!"

"What!"

"Get off!"

"I'm not getting off!"

"Get off! I can't steer!"

"I just got on. I'm not getting off. I'm not getting back in the water."

Later, I learned Linda—my loving companion of 25 years—was contemplating knocking me off the bow with her paddle.

Eventually, we worked as a team. I climbed off—although still clinging to the kayak—and we made our way downstream to a spot where we could land.

I scrambled up the bank.

There I stood: naked, shaken, cold, withered, trembling.

"Put this on," she said, tossing my T-shirt to me. "Stay here."

Where was I going?

Linda hiked away through the trees, making her way upstream.

Cold as I was, I put the T-shirt on like I always do.

She recovered my kayak and paddle and returned to where I was standing, shivering. She pulled the kayak out of the water and stared at me in disbelief. "Not like that!"

"What? I'm cold."

"On the bottom. Put your legs through the arms."

So, I did, and there I stood in my T-shirt trunks.

Eventually, each in our own kayak, we continued, and soon we were in sight of the office. Well before those rapids we had seen in the morning, we pulled our kayaks out of the water.

"I'll be back with clothes." And Linda hiked off.

Standing alone, waiting, with large bruises from my shoulders to my broken toenails, I looked like an old Holstein bull—in a diaper.

At last, Linda arrived in her SUV. With clothes. Wonderfully warm clothes.

Amazingly, we had returned with all the equipment we had rented.

It has been months now. The bruises are gone, but my ribs still hurt, and kayaking memories remain.

I wish I could show you some photos, but of course, the camera is in the pocket of my trunks, in the North Fork of the White River, heading for Arkansas.

I now own a pair of water shoes—just in case—although I have no kayaking plans anytime soon.

Maybe next summer.

My Brother

Georgia Sparks

I DON'T REALLY REMEMBER the last time I saw him. It had to be on one of his many trips back home after being on the racing circuit. I have an old family photo that was taken in front of my sister's house. That may have been the last time he came to see us—the last time I saw him or spoke to him.

He was seven years older than I, but thanks to home movies, I have memories of him as a boy. I watched as that skinny, fair-haired boy pulled weeds in our backyard. I watched as he walked us to and from school. I watched as he hula hooped at my birthday party. He could hula hoop better than anyone I knew.

As a child he was asthmatic, and while I don't remember him ever having an asthma attack, I do remember him tying a handkerchief over his mouth and nose, like a cowboy bandit, to keep from breathing dust. Our home was in Phoenix, so there was plenty of dust around. When he was called for the draft, he smoked cigarettes to trigger his asthma. It worked--he was 4-F and avoided the military and Vietnam.

My memories are scattered when I think of my childhood years. Actual memories are intermingled with stories of my brother's adventures. Times were tough then, so my crafty Mom made earrings out of rick-rack and sent my brother out to sell them in the neighborhood. The few extra dollars from earring sales helped buy milk. A boy could go out and sell door-to-door in those days without being abducted or threatened by gangs or drugs.

I vividly remember the time he asked to have his hair cut in a mohawk. My parents, though less than enthused about the idea, gave in to his request. The mohawk was not at all attractive, and his hair was soon buzzed to the scalp to remedy the mistake. Even a bald head was better than that haircut.

Because of our age difference, he was in his last year at elementary school when I was in first grade. I saw him at school only if he was working as a patrol boy or cafeteria helper. Whether he was the crossing guard walking us younger kids across the street after school or wiping off tables in the cafeteria during lunch hour, it always felt special being around him.

He moved away from home when he was 16 and went to live on a ranch in Prescott. Because of his small stature, he was encouraged during his childhood to become a jockey. That seed of an idea grew and motivated him to go to work on a horse ranch. He lived in a tack room, mucked stalls, and learned everything he could about horses.

Eventually, he became a jockey. He was good at it and did very well for himself right out of the gate. In a short while, he earned enough to pay cash for a brand new 1965 Ford Fairlane 500. I still recall the day he drove it to our house where he painstakingly installed clear vinyl seat covers over the white leather seats. He also painted the whitewalls on the tires black--though I never really understood why.

During racing season, he traveled to various cities in the United States and Canada. We were excited when racing season opened in our city because we would have his company for a while. And as an added bonus, since he had limited space in his travel trailer, he downsized his music collection and gave us the record albums he was tired of listening to.

I wrote letters to him in those early days. It was a geography lesson just keeping up with his travels: Spokane, Washington; Wilkes-Barre, Pennsylvania; Toronto, Ontario; Calgary, Alberta; Saskatoon, Saskatchewan. I remember receiving letters from him, too. I'm sure he knew how much he was missed.

My dad was extremely proud and really came alive when my brother was back in Phoenix to race. Dad would go to the racetrack in the wee hours on Sunday mornings to watch him gallop horses. My sister and I would sometimes go along on those cold, dark mornings, but we spent more time sitting in the coffee shop drinking hot chocolate than actually watching my brother ride.

Today he would be in his seventies. I sometimes wonder what he would have done with his life had he lived. Jockeys have a short window of time for their career before they are too old to race. I don't know if he had learned any other skills. Jockeying and horses were his whole life.

I guess it should be no surprise that his life ended on a racetrack. The story goes that he was riding a horse, as he had done no doubt thousands of times before, when the horse veered into the guardrail. My brother was thrown from the horse. He was only 34 years old, but he died doing what he loved.

The funeral was held in another state and set for the very day that I was scheduled to have a C-section delivery. Needless to say, I couldn't attend my brother's funeral. But as my wonderful brother whom I dearly loved was being laid to rest, another young man whom I dearly love entered this life. There was this gift in my arms; my firstborn son. I felt somehow that my brother was replaced, and the loss didn't seem nearly so great. Maybe that's the cycle of life. In my experience, it's more than just a cliché.

James Gardener 2.0

D. August Baertlein

The old man hobbled to the receptionist's desk, knees crackling. "I got this free Neo-Physician coupon slipped under my door," he said.

The woman cocked her perfect face to one side and aimed kaleidoscope eyes at him, then turned to read words suspended in midair. Words he couldn't see.

"James Gardner, ninety-four." She turned back. "You've been avoiding us, James."

"Yeah, well. Last time…" James pushed his glasses up the sweaty slope of his nose. "I was having trouble typing on those mini-keyboards and you sharpened my damned fingertips!" He waggled ten pencil-point digits at her. "Bloody things ache when it rains."

"That was ten years ago. Finger-Points are old technology." She laughed. "So is typing. Now we can interface you directly to the InterWeb's, brain to Artificial Intelligence, better known to most as A-I."

James sighed. "Just the knees, please." He wasn't getting burned again.

The receptionist read on. "Oh, James." She tsked. "You should have come sooner. We can do so much more than knees. Eyes." She nodded at his glasses. "Hair. Skin." She cringed at his sagging jawline.

James clicked his fingertips together. "Just make my knees stop hurting."

"We can make everything stop hurting," she said. "Eliminate pain forever."

"That sounds…"

"Great?"

"Too good to be true," he said.

"Oh, it is!" she said. "So good. Our complete neural system transplant replaces your congenital wetware with brand new, silicon-fiber neurons, eliminating all pain."

James shifted his weight from left knee to right.

"Congenital wetware?" he said. "You make it sound like it was diseased from birth?"

"Exactly." She pushed a Hover-Chair up behind him. "Sit." (He had little choice.) She handed him a drink in a cut crystal glass.

The juice was sweet and cold, so tasty he drank it all in one swig. The Hover-Chair nestled softly around him and he began to dose, his eyelids fluttering shut, his thoughts dissolving to fuzz. He was almost asleep.

"James, we meet at last." A man's voice boomed in front of him, but James couldn't open his eyes to locate the source.

"Coupon," the receptionist gloated. "Under his door. He never saw the CyberMail we sent all these years. Probably didn't know he had an account."

"Ha!" said the doctor. "Well, we'll upgrade the old boy now. He's been an unsightly, bumbling drain on society long enough." He paused. "Eyes, hair, skin, neural system…"

'Just knees!' James tried to scream.

"Oh, wait!" said the doctor, and for a moment James was relieved, but only for a moment. "We can upload his consciousness directly into one of those new robo-bodies."

The receptionist clapped. "Yes. And we'll upgrade his mental acuity while we're at it."

Mr. Bow Tie

Dolores Everard-Comeaux

I'D BEEN SUFFERING FROM a dratted writer's block and ducking the muse that feeds creativity for some years. I always planned to return to writing once I reached retirement. Time yelled, "How in heavens can you work writing into your crazy schedule? What about the *block*?"

The ANTS (anxious negative thoughts) in my brain blared. Green toxic words slid between neurons and tickled my amygdala to form Nervous Nelly thoughts. Ageism touted, "Thinking's not sharp enough. Spelling sucks. Shorterm memory *kaput*! Long-term memory short."

"*Sha Bebe,* listen up!"

That got my attention. It appears my muse speaks Cajun French and has signed on to squash the ANTS. She whispered gently, "Don't pay attention to rules and regulations of writing for the draft. Remember what your editor at the newspaper said years ago: "Just write. Keep writing."

What a trip that was writing for my hometown daily rag. My incredible editor, Preston L. Pendergrass, whipped my dangling participles into shape, found my misplaced modifiers, and beat into my brain journalistic jargon. He actually forgave my grammatical goofs like "petro" for gasoline and "ladies" for women. He commented that not all women were ladies. In our hometown, he was considered a master grammarian.

What a character! He was as regular as a clock at his desk each morning, clad in a stiff, starched white shirt. It was punctuated by a bright bow tie clamped for dear life to his collar. Sometimes, I imagined the bow tie to be a red helicopter landing on that stiff collar. My desk faced his office door. Often, I sneaked a peek to see him pecking away with two fingers on an old manual typewriter at warp speed.

For as gruff as he sometimes seemed, he had a warm and squishy heart. I was a single mother of two and had put their Christmas on layaway early in the fall to penny-pinch and pay it out coin-by-coin. The day before Christmas Eve, I went on my lunch hour to the department store to retrieve their Santa. To my horror, I found that the store had put the tiny black and white TV, plus a couple of other small items, back on the shelf. I returned to the newsroom in tears. The song," A Hard Rock Candy Christmas," played in the back of my mind. I told the editor my tale of woe then scooted back to my desk. Tears trickled past my nose, as red as Rudolph's.

Almost immediately, the department store called that they had replaced my meager presents. It occurred to me that my editor might have clout in the community and that tie stuck to his collar was really bright red angel wings.

As obit editor, one time I mucked up and buried a person in an opposite cemetery to where the burial was to be held (there were two cemeteries in our hometown). The family came storming in to kill me. The editor with the bright bow tie invited the couple into his office for a "crucial conversation." I had already started cleaning out my desk, certain of being fired and wondering how to make ends meet with little income. In fact, I had the boys on free meals at school, and the newspaper had given them bright red windbreakers with the name of the daily rag boldly stated on the back. These jackets saved me a few needed bucks in the coat department. They may have been an embarrassment to the boys, since no other kids wore bright red windbreakers with *The Baytown Sun* blazoned on the back.

A burial miracle! The upset couple left the editor's office with a promise of rerunning the obit correctly. I wasn't fired. However, I remained under the editor's scrutiny. His persistent and patient mentorship taught me the trade. More than journalism, I learned the power of forgiveness and that it's okay to mess up. After all, we humans are messy mortals at times.

I owe much to the newsroom and an editor who gave me a trade and encouragement to write. I learned much from this stern character, which could cause my knees to knock and my heart to pound when corrected. But best of all, I received a valuable life lesson from that editor, who donned a bright bow tie that sat a hand-span above an incredibly warm and forgiving heart.

A Christmas Test

D.R. Roe

HER CHILD IS BORN the first of November, just three days after her twentieth birthday. A child herself, she's now responsible for the needs of her infant son.

Nearly a month later, her husband announces he has taken a new job. It's in the city almost one hundred miles away. A week later she finds herself in a new town far from family and all that she has known.

The Christmas holiday brings a blizzard with bitter temperatures, high winds, and heavy snowfall. Her husband has been gone for several days. The job has not turned out as he had hoped. He admitted that the responsibility of a family was more than he could bear. Now alone with her infant son in a strange and unfamiliar place.

She is not surprised by this turn of events. In the two years of marriage, he never did prove himself much of a husband. During her pregnancy, she often wondered of his capabilities as a father.

The stress is beginning to take its toll; having no money, and the meager food supply is nearly gone. The lack of proper nourishment has inhibited her body's ability to produce milk to feed her child. The last thing she wants to do is reach out to her parents for help. The thought of hearing the disappointment in their voice is discouraging.

After washing the cloth diapers by hand, she hangs them around the apartment to dry. She sterilizes the glass bottles in boiling water in order to fill them with sterilized water; her hope is that the water will help satisfy the baby's hunger. The Doctor had said that, if needed, the premixed formula could be used to supplement the baby's diet.

Formula is available at the drug store less than a half mile from the apartment—62 cents a can. "There must be some change around here somewhere," she declares. She searches under the cushions of the sofa, high on shelves, on top of the dresser, in all the drawers, and under every piece of furniture. She finds a total of fifty-nine cents. More is needed.

Although she doesn't know any of the neighbors in her building, from deep within she finds the nerve to knock on their apartment doors to ask for the needed three pennies. No one answers at the first few doors. At the next, the door opens. An elderly woman wearing a plush robe that drags on the floor stands in the doorway. "Yes dear. What is it?"

"Could you please help me? I need three cents. I will pay it back."

"Well, I think I can spare three pennies." The woman pulls the pennies from a bowl of change on a table by the door. "No need to worry about paying it back. Merry Christmas."

"Thank you so much." She pushes the pennies into her pocket.

Back in her apartment, she stuffs the fifty-nine cents in the pocket with the pennies. Outside, the heavy snow is whipping about in the high winds. She wonders if she can battle this monster.

"I'm not sure if I can do this," she mumbles.

It is now 6:30 p.m. The baby begins to cry again. The water worked for only a short time.

After putting on her meager remnant of a coat, she wraps the tiny baby in a warm blanket, and bundles him completely in a quilt, covering his face to protect him from breathing the cold air.

"Here we go, Little Bit. We'll get you something to eat real soon."

Approaching the outer door of the building, she swallows her fear and pushes it open. The wind snatches it, slamming the door against the outside wall of the building.

"You have to be kidding me!"

She tries to grab hold of the door with her one free arm, but the wind is so strong she can't move it. Grumbling in disgust while struggling with all of her body weight to close the door against the force of the wind.

On the descent down the icy steps, she grasps tightly to the railing to keep upright. In the parking lot she can more easily balance her weight. She presses her precious cargo snugly to her chest. Her only thought is to forge ahead in spite of the storm.

It is impossible to see more than a few feet because of the heavy snow. She has to squint her eyes, lean forward, and push headfirst through the pommeling conditions.

The bitter wind slices through her worn torn coat, burning her skin. She looks up with hopes of seeing the lights of the shopping plaza in the distance. But there is only darkness. The snowflakes sting as they hit her face.

Before long, her body feels weary and begins to ache. Every muscle beseeches her to give up. But there is no shelter. It is imperative to press on, although feeling like she's been walking forever. She then sees the lights above the drug store faintly peeking through the heavy snow.

"I can see the sign," she murmurs to her son. "It's kind of blurry, but we're getting closer."

A ray of hope shines, rousing every bit of strength within to step up the pace in anticipation of getting to the phone booth that stands at the outside corner of the parking lot.

Once inside, she closes the door between them and the unyielding tempest. Inside the booth is a small shelf, just the right size to set her bundle on.

"Wow! Check it out, Little Bit, it's just your size."

Arms weakened, they hang limp at her sides.

"Thank you, Lord, for this shelter where I can rest awhile. And thank you for this perfect spot to lay my baby on."

The only lights that shine throughout the shopping plaza are from inside the drug store. It is the only store open on this Christmas Eve. Approaching the store, she sees a few cars parked in front, proclaiming she is not the only one out on this night.

As she opens the door, a blast of heat from inside smacks her in the face. Upon stepping inside, the warmth engulfs her as if stepping into a cloud.

Once she finds the section where the formula is shelved, she sets her bundle on the floor and unwraps the blankets that envelope the child. He had not stirred since leaving the apartment. The young mother fears the worst. Has she smothered him by clutching him too tightly?

As she lifts the blanket that covers his face, the shock knocks her back from her squatted position onto her buttocks. These eyes looking back at her are not the eyes of her infant son. These are wise eyes that seem to hold all the knowledge of the universe. Mesmerized, she is unable to look away, for what seems to be several minutes. She has the feeling that he is inhabited by an angel traveling with them on their journey. And they seem to be totally aware of what she is experiencing.

Breaking away from the trance like state, she turns her attention to the task at hand. She looks for a can of premixed formula, but there are none to be seen. Frantically shifting about all the items on the shelf, she cries, "No! There must be one. Please!"

Then, obscurely placed in the back on the top shelf, hidden behind other items, she finds a can of premixed formula. It is a far stretch to reach the lone can.

"Thank you, Lord!"

Scooping up the baby she hurries to the cashier, pulls the change from her pocket, and places it on the counter next to the can. The clerk rings up the purchase.

"Exact change. Thank you and have a Merry Christmas."

Hating to leave the cozy warmth of the store, she wraps the baby and the can together in the blanket. While exiting, snow blows in the open doorway. Conditions outside seem worse than before.

After taking advantage of a short pause at the phone booth, she again sets out into the snow squall. Soon the lights from the shopping plaza are blotted out and darkness is the backdrop for the heavy snowstorm. The howling, blustering wind whirls the intense snowfall about her, yet she walks effortlessly as if she is surrounded by a protective bubble.

Upon entering the apartment, she catches the reflection of herself in the mirror hanging by the door. She is surprised to see there is not a single snowflake adorning her hair or coat. The blanket covering the baby is also dry.

"How can this be?" she utters in amazement.

Because she had no tree decorated with tinsel and lights, she lights a candle in celebration of Christmas Eve. Later nestled in the rocking chair feeding her baby, she gazes at the flickering flame with a smile of gratitude and affirms,

"You know, Little Bit, I think a Christmas Angel helped us tonight. I believe we are going to be just fine. Merry Christmas."

Personal Essay:

More Eggs & Tomatoes

Darlis Sailors

AS A CHILD I USED TO think being kind was not fighting with my brothers, not being selfish with my toys or not grabbing the last cookie on the plate. But as I grew older, my understanding broadened.

To be kind meant to be concerned about others, not as one big *do-all* but in *little seeds of kindness* every day.

Positive seeds/deeds can be scattered about, unnoticed by anyone but those who need them. Kindness might be an encouraging word to the weary, or a cup of coffee and a listening ear. It could be a card that says *Thinking of You*, or anything done to meet a specific need that won't let go of your heart.

Kindness can turn up in an act so small that you don't even remember doing it. Some people call it "doing a good turn."

In our early-married years, we began full-time ministry in a small church with a growing congregation. My husband was their first associate pastor. His salary was small, but housing was also provided.

The budget was tight, and utilities were high. We shut off two of the bedrooms to create more efficient use of the living room wall heater. Living near the church eased car expenses, but parishioner kindness had a great impact on the budget, too.

One of the founding families started bringing us homegrown tomatoes and a flat of eggs. We received them joyfully. One time as I was thanking them, the husband said, "We drive to an egg ranch up in the hills and it's just as easy to buy two flats as one." They continued their kindness for several years.

We left that church and moved out of state; however, ten years later they called asking us to return for further ministry. By then the church had really grown, but it was nice to see the family that had been so kind to us in our early years.

We were excited to tell them how their constant supply of eggs and tomatoes had blessed us. But much to our surprise, they said they did not remember doing that.

There may be no reason for you to remember your good deeds; however, they may remain forever in the mind of those who experience them.

We have never forgotten those eggs and tomatoes. In fact, those *seeds of kindness* have born much fruit over the years because we have tried to repay them by *paying it forward*.

Personal Essay

Better Than Sex

Elaine Greensmith Jordan

I SAT ALONE in my office one morning, enjoying the view outside my window—a desert scene of manzanita brush and wildflowers—thinking of my Sunday sermon about the ***New Testament*** story when Jesus transformed water into wine at a wedding in Cana.

Startled at the sound of a knock at the church door, I opened it to a small man in grimy clothes.

"Where's the preacher?" he asked. "I got these troubles. Need money." He scratched his shaded chin, looking like a grizzled character in a western movie.

"I'm the minister here," I said, smiling and feeling pleased to help out a man of the Wild West. "I can offer you some—"

He took a step back, as if confronted by the evil eye. "You ain't no minister! I wanna see the *real* minister!"

"I assure you—"

"You're a *woman,* for Christ's sake!" he shouted and stepped back further.

I held on to the doorjamb, trying to look clerical. "Well, yes, but I'm the minister of this church, and—"

"I know why this church is going to hell, *lady*," he shouted from his safe distance. "It's because of people like *you*!" His weathered face watched me as if waiting for me to levitate. We stood unmoving until he wandered away.

Sitting at my desk, I felt a dark pain press against my forehead. People like that poor tired cowboy, I thought, take me to be a sorceress. How could he? I'm a plain schoolteacher type, brown eyes behind glasses.

I took a long gulp of cold coffee, restoring my dented courage. What in God's name am I doing in ministry? Water into wine is harder than I thought. I sighed and heard another knock. Feeling some misgivings, I opened the door to Charlotte, a church member who stood holding a chocolate cake. She was smiling. The contrast with my former visitor made me smile too.

"They say it's a 'Better than Sex' cake," she said.

"Did you bring any wine?" I asked, enjoying the look on her face.

Second Chance

Melody Huttinger

ANNE STARED IN THE MIRROR one more time, fixed an imagined lipstick smudge and smoothed her hair. She huffed. For cripes sake, get over yourself. It's just coffee, not a date to the opera. She grabbed her purse and started for the door but couldn't resist one last look at her full-length image. Ugh, the trendy skinny jeans drew attention to her newly acquired muffin top. Damn the holidays!

She'd always been slim, but it was harder to keep the weight off now that she was officially an old person. Past sixty qualified for being old, didn't it? In spite of the hip sayings—forty is the new thirty and so on, she didn't truly believe sixty was the new fifty. At least her knees didn't believe it. Still, she looked pretty darn good for her age. At least that's what her friends told her. Of course, it was possible they were lying to make her feel good.

Now she had to change clothes, for the third time. With a grunt, she lifted one leg to tug off her tall spike-heeled boots (a recent purchase, along with the skinny jeans), ended up collapsed in a tangle onto the carpeted floor.

The door opened, and her husband of twenty-nine years poked his head in.

Joe grinned. "Whataya doing down there? Trying out a new yoga pose?"

"Very funny. Now pull me up." When upright, Anne hobbled over to the bedroom chair with one boot half on, sat and held up her feet. "Can you help, please?"

"Sure thing." He grabbed the fashion footwear and eased them off. "Need anything else, Annie? I'm heading to the dock to help Jerry paint his boat."

"No, have fun." Typical Joe. He was always helping one of his many friends do something. He hadn't even asked what she was doing. And that was exactly why she was going on this rendezvous. Benign neglect. Most of their conversations included his beloved boat or what was on the menu for dinner.

As the door closed on her husband, Anne scurried across the room and rushed into the large walk-in closet. She unzipped the jeans and with difficulty, peeled them down, ending up breathless from the effort. Who came up with such a stupid thing as skinny-jean, anyhow? If you were past thirty, they made you look like a frog with pockets. She surveyed the row of hanging trousers and chose a black pair with and an elastic waistband. So much for trying to look young and cute.

Ignoring the stylish boots, Anne reached for sensible flats. Better than breaking an ankle for the sake of impressing an old flame with her youthfulness. Anne rechecked her lipstick and re-combed her blond bob. At least her hair looked good. No gray—only her hairdresser knew for sure and Miss Clairol wouldn't tell. She glanced at her watch. Got to get going. It was a good thing she'd started getting ready two hours early.

Stuck in traffic twenty minutes later, Anne wondered just when her smallish town had morphed into a nightmare of waiting through two or three light changes every day. Damn the tourists!

As the minutes slowly ticked by, Anne began doubting whether her escapade was ethical or even moral. Maybe she shouldn't go through with it. There was still time to turn the car around. No harm, no foul. After all, she hadn't seen Sean in thirty years, until the chance meeting when she'd been out with her girlfriend, Karen, last week.

She'd recognized him immediately, sitting across the room in the Coffee Clash Café. He hadn't changed much, still handsome and fit looking. His hair black as a raven's wing, just like she remembered. It was a little odd, but then some people didn't seem to age.

A tennis racquet lay on the seat next to him. He'd been a pro when she knew him, and throughout the years, articles in the paper would report his victories in exotic locales. Hometown boy makes good and all that. He probably wouldn't even remember her. But man did she remember him.

Anne was plotting how to casually run into Sean when he stood and headed for the exit. She leapt out of her chair, and sprinted for the door, 'accidentally' bumping into him.

"Sean!" she'd said like she'd just noticed him, and not been surreptitiously salivating for the last half hour. "Do you remember me? We dated way back when."

"Hey, Sugar! How could I forget you?" He gave her a peck on each cheek, European style. "I have a court reserved right now, but let's get together sometime. Give me your number."

She fumbled around in her purse for a pen, but he pulled out his cell phone. "What is it? I'll put it in right now."

Feeling stupid and hopelessly out of date, she muttered the digits to him. He flashed her a movie star smile and dashed out the door.

After he fled, Karen walked over and gave her a sly look. "Was that Sean O'Conner? You practically knocked him over with your exuberance." She smiled. "Don't blame you—he's still a total hunk."

Anne felt her cheeks inflame. "I just wanted to say hello."

Karen patted her arm. "It's okay by me. Frankly, I always was surprised you chose Joe over Mr. Wonderful."

Anne jumped to her husband's defense. "Joe's a good man, great father, and—."

Karen laughed. "And hopelessly predictable."

On the way home from that fateful meeting, Anne convinced herself Sean would never phone. And that was for the best. She was happily married, well, mostly happily married. Joe had a paunch, (not an all-out beer belly) and was losing his hair, (not as bald as a ping pong ball) and was way too settled into the retirement lifestyle, (besides his friends, and the boat, only interested in the game on weekends). When he remembered she was there at all, it was to order another beer or more chips. It turned out, their plans of traveling the world after they both retired was her dream, not his. Damn ESPN!

Back when they were both twenty-nine, Anne met Joe at a party. Tall, average looking, and kind of bookish. Not her type at all, but she was between boyfriends and they began doing things together. To her surprise, she fell for him, hard. They had one blissful summer, the best of her life. For the first time, Anne was in love and began making plans to tie the knot.

One-night Joe took her to a romantic bluff overlooking the city and she was positive he would pop the question. She wiggled close, and he said, as if he were continuing the conversation, "so I'll be leaving tomorrow for the city. The specialized training, they offer is essential for my career." He never mentioned marriage or even pursuing a long-distance relationship. Anne was too stunned for words.

That night her world crumbled and fell to dust at her feet, but dignity wouldn't allow her to cry and carry-on about it in front of him. She was a big girl, and relationships ended. That's the way it was. It was simply a summer romance and now it was over. Kaput.

After wallowing in self-pity for an entire week, Anne forced herself to go to happy hour with Karen. They were drinking and laughing, (a glass of wine or two makes everything better) when a meltingly handsome guy stopped by their table.

"Hi, I'm Sean," he said to Anne, ignoring Karen. "I haven't seen you here before. Would you like to go out sometime?"

Anne blinked and stammered, "I . . . I don't know." The abandonment by Joe was still raw, but then she thought, why not? She took a breath and said, "Yes, I would."

His fabulous smile lit up the dim room. "Great!" He wrote down her number, (that was before cell phones), and said he'd call her in a day or so.

The day or so turned out to be more than a week, and Anne had nearly forgotten the incident when her phone jingled, and it was Sean. They began dating. He was fun and attentive, and always dropped her a postcard when he was on tour. But he wasn't Joe.

Anne told Sean about Joe, but instead of putting him off, it seemed to make him more determined than ever to win her. She gradually felt her shattered heart mending, and Sean began looking better and better. He was getting pretty serious, and there was nothing not to like. He made great money, traveled to exciting places and kept in touch.

After a few months of a whirlwind courtship, he presented her with a one-carat diamond.

"Flawless, just like you, Sugar," he'd said.

It was the most beautiful thing she'd ever seen, but since her breakup with Joe, it was hard to contemplate marriage. She stalled. Sean was about to leave on another trip, and Anne promised to have an answer upon his return.

Then Joe showed up. Just like that, no phone call, no letter, no nothing, just showed up on her stoop. She opened the door and he was standing there, flowers in hand, grinning like he had all the numbers on the Powerball ticket. The old feeling rushed back, and Anne nearly fainted from light-headedness.

But he wasn't getting off that easy.

"It's been months! You can't just waltz in after all this time and expect me to fall all over myself." Anne began closing the door. "Besides, I have a new boyfriend."

Joe put his foot out, effective as a door jam. There was a long silence as they stared at each other through the crack. Finally, he said quietly, "I thought we had an understanding. I only took that training, so I could get a promotion into management. Now we'll have enough money to get married, Annie."

Her knees wobbled like Jell-O. "Married? You should have clued me in."

He swallowed. "I could've sworn we talked about this."

Typical Joe. He always thought they talked about things, but mostly it was in his head. Smart, funny, good-hearted, clueless. That was her Joe.

They were married the following weekend, and when Sean returned from his tennis tournament, Anne had the difficult task of telling him she was married. He took it well, considering. She heard that within a couple of months, he was engaged to someone else. Anne preferred to believe it was a rebound situation and not a character flaw.

Life was good during the intervening years of settling into family life and raising children. Not exciting, but good. Every once in a while, though, Anne couldn't help but wonder, what if? Especially when she saw the sports page with a picture of Sean trouncing his opponent by serving an ace ball. Or partying with the jet set. Or meeting the Prince of Monaco. She could've had a life of adventure, met famous people, gone to galas on the arm of a delicious guy to the envy of every other woman in the room. Instead, she had Joe.

So, when Anne ran into Sean that day, it almost seemed like a second chance. Not that she really expected him to phone. Thirty years was a long time. He was probably married, too. But the very next day, he did call and asked her out for lunch. She'd hesitated, then said, "How about coffee? We can meet at the Coffee Clash."

At last the traffic eased and Anne wheeled into the café lot. Shoot, it was full. She spotted a slot across the street and after several attempts, maneuvered her full-sized SUV into it, all the time wondering why she hadn't bought that Mini Cooper.

She was so near to the next car, Anne had to suck in her stomach to squeeze out. After the close encounter with the door, she straightened her clothes and walked to the cafe, glad she didn't have to negotiate the uneven pavement in her spike-heeled boots.

Sean, sitting at an outside table, stood and pulled out another chair when he saw her. "Hope this is okay. Reminds me a little of Paris."

Anne's heart hammered. What she wouldn't give to actually be in Paris. With him. She sat, and he helped her chair in. She sighed. Just as gentlemanly as she remembered. "It's good to see you, Sean."

"You, too, Sugar."

She smiled. His pet name for her.

A pretty, twenty-something waitress showed up with her pad and pencil ready. After ordering them both Non-fat Lattes with a double shot, Sean gave the girl a seductive smile and said, "Thanks, Sugar."

Anne almost choked on her sip of water. 'Sugar' was his special name for *her*, not some random barista. Did he even *remember* her real name? He hadn't used it even once. She swallowed her disappointment and said, "It's been a long time, you must be married by now."

"Not at the moment. In the middle of a messy divorce."

"That's too bad, after so long. Didn't you get married right after we broke up?"

Sean looked blank for a moment. "Oh, not *that* wife. There's, uh, been a few since then."

"A few?"

"Well, only four."

"You've been married *four* times?"

"Five, including the first one. But I don't usually include her because we were both so young, and it only lasted a couple of months." He began counting off on his fingers. "The second one didn't understand me, the third was a total bitch, the fourth was boring and this last one is completely crazy."

While Anne sat dumbfounded, Sean rattled on about the horrible women he'd been involved with. When she managed to ask about children, he went off about how his one son, at seventeen, had run away to Los Angeles to become a devoted Steampunk fan.

He complained about the loneliness of life on the road and then groused about returning to his hometown to teach tennis skills to old ladies. Sean had nothing good to say about anyone or anything. He never asked one question about her life, not even if she was married.

And throughout this non-stop tirade, Anne's eyes kept revisiting the part in his hair. Could it be? Yes, definitely. The telltale sign of gray roots.

Was this the same person from so long ago? When had he become so thoroughly self-absorbed or had he always been that way and she didn't recognize it? Anne felt trapped by his diatribe but couldn't find an excuse to exit without seeming rude. The boredom became complete after fifteen minutes, but she endured the harangue for another ten before she'd had enough. She stood abruptly and gathered her purse.

He put his hand on her arm. "I'll call you soon, and we can go play, like old times," he said, flashing bleached-white teeth.

She shook off his hand. "Sorry, better not. My husband wouldn't like it." Anne felt instant gratification at the stupefied stare he gave her and walked away without a backward glance.

Joe was home for lunch by the time she got there, fixing himself a grilled cheese sandwich. "Can I make you one, Annie?"

"Sounds good." She plopped down at the kitchen island and noticed a travel brochure. "What's this?" she asked, picking it up. The cover read *Paris and The Wine Country of France*.

"For our trip next month. I just picked up the tickets from the travel agent."

Anne's jaw nearly hit the floor. "What trip?"

Joe blinked. "We talked about it, right?"

She ran to him, laughing, and snuggled into his arms. "Typical Joe."

The Story Ranch

Amber Polo

THE CABIN WASN'T CHARMING or particularly cute, just a step up from ordinary. Didn't even look particularly lived in. Her map indicated the Story Ranch was the only building in the vast Story Desert.

Rumors told her that burying her story would lift memories from her mind and heart. She'd be able to sleep and go on with her life. She hurried around to the back field. She wanted this over. She had to be rid of it.

Behind the cabin, she saw piles of soft dirt as if an army of gophers had advanced to attack the cabin. She couldn't falter now. Choosing a serviceable spade from an assortment of shovels, she began to dig in an untouched spot. The ground was hard. But no harder than she'd expected. Leaning her entire weight on her shovel, at last the blade broke the surface and she lifted out a scoop of brown sandy dirt. A few more shovelfuls and the hole was a foot deep.

She removed a think stack of papers from her bag, placed them in the hole, and smoothed them flat. Refilling the hole with a sigh, she stomped down the dirt, turned, and left with a step lighter than she'd felt in years.

≈≈≈≈

A few hours after the woman left, a man walked into the field. Looking over his shoulder, he moved quickly, following what he called his Inspiration, took up his regular shovel, strode to the freshest mound of dirt, and uncovered the papers. Holding the sheets up, he shook off the remaining earth. There were few rules here, but the one that could not be broken was that once he touched the pages he couldn't put them back, nor could he return for a year and a day. But he'd learned to trust his first judgment and today as he scanned the first page, knew he'd chosen well. This woman's story would become a bestselling novel like all his others.

Jesus in the Kitchen

Lena Hubin

HE HUNG IN an oval frame on an oblique wall in our Iowa kitchen. Wavy brown hair caressed his shoulders; his warm dark eyes looked toward a far corner of the ceiling.

I faced him from my place at the round oak table as we ate. "I fold my hands, I bow my head; I thank thee, Lord, for this good bread," we said, and as I lifted my young head from the prayer, I wondered: Was Jesus responsible for the bread my mom slapped into being each Saturday with her fine-boned hands? If so, how?

"Jesus loves me," this I was supposed to know, according to the song, but the Bible never did tell me so—at least not so I'd believe it. With those Middle-Eastern eyes of his, JC gazed upward, dark and golden-aura'd—consumed by reverence, and heedless of the likes of me.

He was *Mom's* Jesus, this guy on the wall, not mine. I know Mom loved him. She'd hung his portrait; she went to church and prayed "in Christ our Lord." And she'd married my dad, who was JC's spitting image, with shorter hair—a dark-haired, dark-eyed, gentle farmer.

But I would seek and find that same soft, raw-umber allure in men whom I'd love fiercely. The first was dark, soulful-eyed Richard Cohen, whom as a teen I dreamed in vain of kissing beneath the pines during ice-skating parties. In Arizona, Armando Garcia's chiseled cheekbones drew me into many kisses before he told me he was married. I met handsome, charismatic Raj Patel at a San Francisco party; we married within a month, and two years later we divorced.

Just like mom's, none of my JC look-alikes had stuck.

Serene and silent, always looking the other way, neither Jesus nor any of his facsimiles would ever know me, nor I them. I traded them off for a lasting relationship with a tall, talkative, flaxen-haired Scandinavian who looked my way and smiled, showing his white, even teeth.

When Mom died, Dad left Jesus hanging on the bedroom wall of their little house in town. The oval portrait was there when he passed nine years later, and it fell to me to figure out what to do with it. I had it in a Goodwill pile till Aunt Jean, Mom's sister, came by and claimed it for her bedroom wall. Her husband—gruff, dark-haired Uncle Reuben—had died from heart problems a few years before. I suspect Jesus has taken his place.

Unexpected Grace

Joanne Sandlin

HURRIEDLY GRABBING A CARTON of Rocky-road ice cream, I almost ran into a young woman and an older couple turning into the frozen food aisle. I paused to avoid a collision. The man clutched his wife tightly to provide a steadying arm.

I saw the familiar face of someone with the blank stare of dementia as well as her choppy gait. I smiled at the trio as they nodded appreciating the opportunity to pass easily. The man dropped behind as the younger woman gripped the older lady picking up the pace to move her along.

He said to me, "My wife needs to get quickly to the restroom."

I asked if she was well. He dropped his eyes replying, "She has dementia."

I told him I experienced that in my family and understood the difficulties it brings daily.

He then stood upright proudly stating, "My name is Lester and I am 91 years old."

His smile reflected his joy in that accomplishment.

"Lester, I am so glad to meet you. I wish I had a big button you could wear saying how young you are."

His even bigger smile affirmed his obvious delight in my interest.

Sensing he might, I asked him if he happened to know the Lord. Looking at me seriously, he related, "If I didn't know Him, I couldn't have made it all these years as well as not being able to carry on with my dear wife's illness."

"God's grace is truly sufficient for us just as He promises in his word, isn't it?"

"Yes, from the day we accept Him into our life through all the peaks and valleys we experience on the journey, He is right there with the grace we need for each circumstance."

"Amen, Lester, what a great testimony."

His easy smile again lit up his face.

The women appeared, and Lester turned quickly with a wave of his hand and joined them.

Moving my cart to the checkout stall I felt blessed to have shared Lester's reminder of God's grace that he carried into every day as he lovingly cared for his wife having experienced it from the day he asked the Lord into his life.

Placing my items on the belt I smiled as I picked up the ice cream pausing to silently thank the Lord for my encounter in the frozen food aisle.

Red Leather Boots

Diane Phelps Budden

RED LEATHER BOOTS! How I wanted a pair. Bright red, flat-soled, fitted below the knees, these red boots were made for dancing—folk dancing. They added excitement and energy to the traditional Hungarian national costume: white tulle blouse with full sleeves and pleated skirt encircled with red and green velvet ribbons; white apron; red velvet vest and "parta" or headdress encrusted with gold braid and decorations. Red, green, and white ribbons, the national colors of Hungary, fluttered down the back of the headdress like birds in flight.

The costumes were worn by the children's folk dance troop at the annual Hungarian Grape Festival. This was back in the days when Cleveland, Ohio, was home to the largest Hungarian community outside of Budapest. The festival was held throughout September and October in Hungarian social clubs and churches in the city. Brought to Cleveland by immigrants around the turn of the century, the festival was held wherever Hungarians settled, much as it was in the "old country." Its peasant roots in Hungary were a celebration of a successful harvest season. Each year, before the traditional folk dancing and soulful violin music began at the festival, and following a custom hundreds of years old, men attached clusters of grapes to wires strung high in the hall's side yard: a veritable cloud of red and purple overhead. Children, and even some mischievous adults, would try and "steal" the grapes without being caught by the "judge," who fined the thieves and embarrassed them as loudly as possible. The money was donated to the church. I remember my tiny grandma Lila, usually quiet and reserved, plucking down grapes that were out of my reach, and barely within hers, as fast as possible. As we made off with our grapes, she would yell encouragement to other would-be thieves, obviously enjoying her role as rogue robber.

My sister and I had willingly agreed to learn the children's folk dances. We would have participated even without my mother's insistence just to have the red leather boots. In the characteristic way of the older child, my sis perfected the energetic steps and twists and turns yelled out by our instructor, while I followed along as best I could. I loved dancing, but I was easily distracted.

I found a photograph of our dance troop among my mother's mementos when she passed away, maybe thirty-five young girls and a smattering of boys. (As usual, the boys chose not to folk dance.) My sister and I are both sitting in the front row of the photo with our hands and ankles crossed like the other girls, very ladylike. My hair is cut short, a rite of passage at our home upon graduation from elementary school after a childhood of braids. My sister smiles happily, not me so much. I suddenly remember I had a spectacular case of poison ivy, especially on the fingers of both hands, slathered with calamine lotion by my mother. I had locked my hands and fingers together as if in prayer and rubbed them back and forth fiercely to alleviate the itching. "You'll only make it worse," my mother pointed out. She was right, of course.

As I study the photo a second time, I muse about my upbringing compared to my own children, influenced as I was by a strong immigrant background. Can only second-or third-generation children experience an ethnic upbringing from the old country?

In her book *The Italian Americans: A History"* author Maria Lautrino presents her view of the immigrant experience: "….an isolated first generation dedicates itself to finding work and raising a family; a more secure second generation, recognizing the chasm between its parents and the culture, seeks to eliminate ethnic traits; and the third and fourth generations set about reclaiming ancestral roots to better define the self…."

The elusive old country—I had no idea at the time it meant my grandma's family farm where she had been born and her family struggled to make a living. She had emigrated 40 years earlier when she was 21 years old with $ 26.00 in her pocket and a trunk-full of belongings. She also brought Hungarian customs and traditions that would help shape me as I grew. Like other immigrants, she was looking for a better life in the golden land of America.

It seems like my grandma always lived with us, upstairs in our two-family house in the city, then in the suburbs where she left her Hungarian community and customs behind. She had a knack for giving the perfect back rub as we talked about the day's events in her room. She used broken English and added Hungarian words for emphasis. She also "read" the comics to me, making up stories to match the images; cooked traditional Hungarian dishes (I've never had authentic strudel since she died); and lectured me on the dangers in the world that she read about in her Hungarian-language newspaper.

My second-generation mother worked hard at distancing us from our heritage. She had spent her childhood looking in from the outside, trying to be as American as possible. She wanted her family to have the

American dream she saw around her. When my sister started school and had pronunciation issues with English, we were banned from speaking Hungarian at home. My sister and I never did speak it again after that—a loss for both of us—but my parents continued to converse in Hungarian with each other when they didn't want us to know what they were saying. (Oftentimes, we could figure it out anyway.)

In the late '50s my parents built a house using the GI bill and moved out of the city to a middle class, very white suburb, as many families did. I ended up chasing my version of the American dream. In our new suburban life, there was no place for grape festivals and folk dances.

My kids experienced a very American, very middle-class upbringing, so I didn't think it was important to share much of the family's immigrant heritage with them. I was wrong about that. I fell into the same trap as my mother and avoided emphasizing my differentness as I was growing up and raising children. Yet, there it was, part of childhood memories that I have come to embrace as I age, as is the wont of the third generation. I think I sensed it wasn't "cool" to be Eastern European in my hometown at that time. Celebrating your roots wasn't in vogue as it is today. I was fully assimilated into white, suburban America and wouldn't have done anything to rock the boat. (Although, I remember when I ran for president of the student council, I used my last name in my campaign posters: "Vote Vajda." *Catchy*, I thought at the time.)

I have many Hungarian treasures passed down through the family: my grandma's beautifully crocheted doilies and dresser scarves; my mother's expert embroidered linens; dishware with folk motifs; Hungarian playing cards; lots of photos of people from the old country that intrigue me. Who were these very serious-looking people in the stark black and white photos? Nobody seemed to know, or I have forgotten what I was told. In one family shot, the man wears an ill-fitting suit, the mother has covered her head with a babushka, and an array of adults and children encircles them. Is this my grandmother's family? On closer examination, the babushka woman could be her mother, and the man her brother—I see a family resemblance.

I wonder if my mom came to miss the Hungarian traditions her mother instilled in her as she grew up. She was always proud to be Hungarian. She did continue some Hungarian traditions. At Christmas, we opened gifts at 12 midnight—timed to miss Santa Claus. She bought us Madame Alexander dolls dressed in the national Hungarian dance costume when we were teens. We were more interested in our high school friends, so the dolls were sold along the way. When she began collecting buttons later in life, she prized the Hungarian buttons she was able to find. She became upset when the meaning and pronunciation of Hungarian words she had used when younger eluded her.

Touring Russia a few years ago with my daughter, I stood in a Moscow subway station, viewing the lovely, elaborate murals and sculptures placed in the stations for the enjoyment of the rush of commuters passing through. At one station, I saw a very colorful, wall-sized mosaic mural of a harvest festival in Ukraine. There were a few folk dancers, easy to pick out in their costumes complete with, yes, red leather boots. I studied the boots closely. One dancer was giving a little kick. I snapped photos of this seemingly happy celebration—you never can tell for sure in Russia—focusing on the red boots that were evidently an important accessory for many Eastern European folk costumes. It was amazing that I had traveled so far from home and the memories of the red boots only to reunite with them once again in Russia.

My red leather boots? I never got a pair. Neither did my sister. My mother couldn't afford to buy them, I guess. I'm sure we made her feel guilty about that. We sure wanted those red leather boots. Funny thing? As I study the dancers in the Hungarian Grape Festival photo, none of the girls are wearing boots, red or otherwise, not even the instructor. They're wearing loafers or Mary Janes, just like me.

My Last Deer Hunt

By Henry Nyal

"Come on," my cousin urged, "you owe it to yourself. And you'll have a real experience as a westerner. Don't be a wussie."

"I don't know," I retorted anxiously, "to kill a wild animal . . ."

"We need the meat, and I know you'll love roast venison—it's the most delicious stuff, and clean. It's natural—no hormones or antibiotics or transfats or crap like that." Wagging his finger in my face, cousin scolded, "the gods made these deer to be enjoyed by protein-deficient college guys, like us. Don't you know it's dangerous to disappoint the gods!"

"With that bit of pagan philosophy, I'm sure I won't go," I said.

"Well, I've got something that'll change your mind," cousin said as he pulled a rifle from behind the divan. "This is our grandpa's thirty-caliber saddle gun, lever action. Uncle Fred lent it to me. Says it has killed many a big buck for the family larder. Told him you were going to get some juicy venison with it."

Cousin handed me the rifle, carefully directing the barrel toward the ceiling. "It's not loaded," he said.

I have to confess I was impressed with this old cattleman's tool. The wooden stock was of fine-grained walnut, comfortably worn and an appealing color. The metal action and barrel were like dark nickel, beautifully finished. The lever action was placed perfectly and had just the right résistance as I shoved it down and pulled it back into place with a solid click. And it had a captivating smell. Was it machine oil or a subtle vapor of burned gunpowder? I was surprised at how familiar this gun felt in my hands, and I realized it was similar in size and weight to the pump action air rifle that I had owned as a teenager. I raised the gun sight and pointed it a fence post outside the window, sighting it confidently, and easing the trigger closed produced a solid click.

"Well?" cousin insisted.

A little embarrassed, I gave in and said, "OK, but you know I probably won't fire it at anything alive."

We made preparations during the week, buying the licenses and day-glow red caps. Throughout the week, I was possessed of a quiet excitement that I refused to acknowledge, even to myself. I liked the old gun.

Saturday, before dawn, we departed for the forest hunting grounds in cousin's old pickup, fresh hunting licenses expectantly nestled in our parka pockets. We parked in a clearing open to the road where three other pickups were already stationed. We strapped on our day packs. In mine, I had a small box of 30 caliber rounds, two boiled eggs, an apple turnover and some plastic bags. I had a small canteen of water on my belt, as well as a new handbook on safe hunting with a rifle. It had a section on dressing out a deer that told me to secure rope, bags and a knife. I had found a few feet of rope and my old pocket knife.

We hiked a mile or so into the forest along a trail that mostly mounted upward, cousin talking about the methodology of finding and killing a deer. It was clear to me that he didn't know much more than I did. After a half hour, he stopped and said we'd better choose a place to meet later, then go in opposite directions because together we'd scare away any deer, making noise walking and talking together.

I headed south along a well-eroded secondary trail. Dawn had come up, so I could see all around clearly. I heard a bird give a shrill cry but couldn't identify the species. After a few minutes, I found myself in a grove of young pines with straight stems, interspersed with scraggly clumps of brush with dark green and gray leaves. I stopped and hunkered down to rest for a moment. My breath hung white in the cold air. I gazed back at the fading trail assuring myself that I could follow it back. I had also brought my ancient Boy Scout compass. The rifle was strapped over my right shoulder which was beginning to ache slightly. An unfamiliar sense of freedom and excitement mixed with anxiety filled me.

As I gazed from tree to tree, an indistinct shape emerged into the grove. It was a deer; no—it was a good-sized buck. I held my breath. He was looking in the other direction as I silently freed the rifle strap from my shoulder. Inch-by-inch I moved the barrel-sight in his direction. *What a magnificent animal!* I thought. From my squatting position, he appeared very large, and I was fixated on the contrasting colors of his tail, underbelly, and face. His nose was dull black, and he stood in what to me seemed a heroic pose. His rack of antlers was impressive, but I didn't try to count the points. A spasm of guilt hit my chest that I calmed as I told myself someone else will kill this buck if I don't---besides we need the food. I had just enough time to disengage the safety switch and aim carefully at his head. I squeezed the trigger. The rifle thundered and jumped in my hands, but the big animal did not cry out or fall. He stood paralyzed, then shook his head violently for at least two seconds before bounding away down the hill.

I was paralyzed for the moment too but seeing he had halted about fifty yards below I followed, trying to move quietly. The buck stood there in profile, so I could see his whole right side. He was vigorously rubbing an antler on a branch. When I reached a spot where I was hidden from him, I felt my hand automatically push down the lever expelling the spent cartridge which flew away. Instinctively I jerk up the lever and a new bullet was inserted into the chamber. The buck flinched at the sharp noises yet continued scrubbing his antler on the branch. The rifle was ready, and I aimed quickly—too quickly. I fired, hitting him again--this time I could see it struck the middle of his gut. He was stopped again for a second in which I worked the lever and fired off another bullet without aiming. This third shot hit him in the rump, in the right hind quarter. He rasped out a cry of pain and tried to run but was reduced to an awkward limp. He headed down again, into a shallow ravine. I followed, running over the broken ground, feeling sick with a realization of the fear and pain my victim must have been feeling. I soon reached him where he had fallen.

He was panting wildly. His wide bright eyes focused on me. Unable to rise and escape he seemed to be begging an answer, why? What have I done to harm you? I pulled down the lever, expelling the empty cartridge casing, feeling a stab of regret that permeated my scalp and the back of my neck. This time I would end his fear and pain. I leaned against the trunk of a larger tree just a couple of yards away and aimed at where I believed his brain would be. With the crack of the shot, his whole body trembled, and his punctured head dropped. Murdered was the first word that went through my brain; I tried to suppress it. Hunting is normal—is human.

As I stared at the inert body, I was impressed by his magnificent rack of horns and observed a big ragged-edged nick where my first bullet had struck. It was weeping blood.

I expelled a full breath and felt the worst of the tension flow away from me with it, leaving only a dead sorrow behind. Looking around, I realized that the big buck and I had descended into a ravine, perhaps a quarter of a mile below the ridgetop where cousin and I had parted. Assessing my victim, I guessed it weighed at least three hundred pounds, and I realized that I had no means to move its heavy body. A small branch projected about six feet up from a tree near where the wounded buck had fallen. I tied its hind limbs together and threw the rope over the branch. Pulling with all my strength, I was able to hang its energy-depleted body up, with only its antlers and head resting on the ground. My pocket knife would hardly pierce the hide. All that meat and I hadn't even prepared myself with the sharp hunting knife.

Sitting on the damp ground, looking in random directions, I didn't know this alien forest. I felt lost—was lost—in so many ways. I understood freshly that I really had not expected success in my hunt.

Give Me Another Drink

Cordell Compton

"I'LL ASK YOU THAT ONCE AGAIN, Officer Parker. How many drinks did you have that night, the night of April 14?"

"A couple, maybe. I don't believe it was more than that."

"Are you sure? Can you be absolutely positive about that statement?"

Officer John Frederick Parker slumped in the chair on the witness stand. He shuffled his feet, clasped his hands and looked at them with focused intensity.

"The Tribunal is waiting, Officer Parker. What is your answer?"

Although he was just barely thirty-five years old, it seemed to the members of the Military Tribunal that the witness had aged visibly before their eyes in recent days. Finally, Parker sat up in the hard, uncomfortable witness chair. Even though the windows were open, the room was stuffy with little cross breeze in the humid and dank air. Cigar smoke drifted around the room and formed a blue haze near the ceiling.

Parker looked up at Assistant Judge Advocate General John A. Bingham who stood less than three feet away.

Bingham leaned on the railing of the witness box that separated the two men.

"I'm sorry, Sir, I cannot be exactly sure how many drinks I had that night. But I don't think I was drunk."

Bingham spun around and glared at the Tribunal's exalted members who were sitting high on the bench in their formal uniforms, medals and battle ribbons hanging on their respective chests like so much wallpaper. He slammed his fist down on the witness box railing with an echoing SMACK that bounced off the walls.

"Don't think you were drunk! What kind of answer is that? What kind of officer are you? Matter of fact, what kind of *man* are you? The biggest responsibility in the world was yours that night. And do you know what?" Bingham's face now was no more than a foot from Parker's. "You failed miserably in those duties, Officer Parker. Dereliction of duty is too kind a phrase to use in your case. Propriety and the high standards of this Tribunal prohibit me from voicing what I really think of you and your actions on the night of April 14. Or should I say your inactions?"

Officer Parker slumped again in the chair. His chest heaved as he groaned and gasped for air. Assistant JAG

Bingham continued to glare at his witness. Perhaps "victim" would be more appropriate.

Major General David Hunter, the Military Tribunal's president, puffed himself up in his chair on the bench. His fellow general and brevet general officers flanked him on either side. Brevet Colonel Horace Porter was the only officer serving on the Tribunal below the rank of general officer.

General Hunter coughed and cleared his throat. "Does the Government have any more questions for this witness?"

Bingham, at last, stepped away from the witness box that encapsulated the demolished form of Officer John F. Parker.

"A closing comment, Sir. Officer Parker, while you are not on trial during these proceedings, if the Government determines there was any dereliction of duty or malfeasance in the performance of your duties, you may, in fact, be subject to a trial to answer for your actions. Do you understand, Officer Parker?" asked Bingham.

Parker slowly nodded his head. Bingham looked down at his witness and for a brief moment, a thin shred of compassion welled within him.

"Let the record reflect that the witness nodded his head in acknowledgment of my statement," said Bingham. "The Government has no further questions."

"Very well, the witness is excused. You may step down," pronounced General Hunter.

Parked reached down and collected his duty cap that earlier had clattered to the floor of the witness box. He nearly tripped getting out of the box and had to quickly grab onto the railing that had separated him from his tormentor during the day's examination. Parker half shuffled, half dragged himself down the aisle and disappeared through the door at the rear of the makeshift courtroom at the Old Capitol Prison. A husky pair of army sergeants acting as bailiffs for the Tribunal closed the door behind Parker.

Major General Hunter rapped his gavel on the bench. "The Tribunal is adjourned for the day. The Tribunal will reconvene tomorrow at 10 a.m."

"All rise," barked another army sergeant standing to the left of the bench. General Hunter and his fellow officers stepped down from the bench and filed out through a side door. As soon as Col. Porter's coattail disappeared through the door, the courtroom cleared instantly.

The Military Tribunal Clerk, George Graham, glanced at the clock over the rear entrance. It was exactly 6:37 p.m. General Hunter had gaveled the session to order that morning promptly at 10:00 a.m. The Clerk noted the time in the Tribunal's Record of Proceedings log book. He tucked the book under his arm and delivered it into the custody of the Master at Arms.

Graham's work for the day was completed. It was long and grinding for him as well as for the rest of those persons in the tight confines of the courtroom. Even so, the day was relatively short compared to other days during the Tribunal's sessions. The testimony was fascinating, dull, insightful and contradictory—often at the same time. Tomorrow was Friday and he eagerly awaited the weekend's respite when the Tribunal was not in session.

During brief breaks in the proceedings during the day, Graham kept thinking to himself: if only Officer Parker had been in the theater that night and had done his duty, the world would surely be different now and this Military Tribunal would not be in session. What if Officer Parker had not weakened in his desire for a drink at that critical moment? What if Parker had stayed at his post? And would he have been able to stop the horrible deed? And what if Charles Forbes, the president's valet, and messenger, had not allowed Booth into the presidential box?

Graham noticed the room had darkened since it was nearly dusk. The day's session ended before the gas jets had to be lit. The approaching darkness matched George Graham's mood as he trudged from the courtroom.

≈≈≈≈≈

Officer John F. Parker gave many hours of testimony that hot June day in 1865 along with several other persons. Parker was not on trial himself but under the withering examination by Bingham, he felt as if he were on trial for his life. In a way, he was.

If someone chose to study Parker's appearance, the person would have difficulty describing him afterward. With a sturdy build and standing several inches over five feet in height, Parker had few distinguishing characteristics. He kept his beard closely trimmed. His dark brown hair did not touch his shirt collar and he always wore a beret regardless of weather. This hypothetical witness would have been forced to describe John Parker with the bland and unhelpful word as; average. Only when he dressed for duty did he assume any outstanding demeanor. The revolver strapped around his waist gave this ordinary man a level of authority.

Parker had a job with the Washington, D. C. Metropolitan Police Department and was assigned as a guard at the White House during the closing days of the Civil War. He accompanied President Abraham Lincoln to Ford's Theater the night of April 14, 1865, when Lincoln was assassinated by John Wilkes Booth. Parker was not an official bodyguard of the president. In fact, Lincoln had no official bodyguards during his presidency in the true sense of the word. At the time, more emphasis was placed on protecting the White House rather than the president himself. Although troops were quartered at the White House during the war, the safety and protection of the president was, at best, casual.

Frequently, Mr. Lincoln rode his horse to the Old Soldiers Home that was near the White House. He enjoyed getting away from the pressures of directing the war efforts for a few hours' respite. He rode at a leisurely gait that allowed him to tip his tall stovepipe hat to well-wishers along the route. During his excursions by carriage when guests or Cabinet officials accompanied him, seldom was there a semblance of any kind of protection save the carriage driver.

After Lincoln was escorted to and seated in his box at the theater on the night of April 14, 1865, Parker left the theater for the Star Saloon next door on 10th Street, N.W., for a drink. He may have had several drinks, but no one really knows for certain. In another tragic oversight Lincoln's valet and messenger, Charles Forbes, allowed Booth into the presidential box. Booth was well known at the theater and had no trouble gaining entrance. Forbes mistakenly assumed that Booth merely wanted to greet the president. Had that event not occurred or if Parker or anyone else had been nearby, Booth might have been stopped or at least hampered in his effort to kill the president.

Along with the other three hundred sixty-five witnesses, Parker was called to testify in the trial of the eight accused conspirators. In the days and weeks after the assassination leading up to the Military Tribunal's proceedings, he began to feel that many persons pointed fingers at him regarding his actions – or "non-actions" as Bingham spat out during his testimony – on the night of the president's murder.

John F. Parker thought he knew his job's duties and believed he had performed them well and yet . . . .?

≈≈≈≈≈

The background of John F. Parker, as we say, was mostly normal –which is to say it was troubled, erratic, unsettled and unguided. John was born May 14, 1830, to

Elias and Mary Parker at their farm in Hagerstown, Maryland. Their farm was modest in size and unpretentious in keeping with other farms in the area. Elias often swelled with pride and false modesty as he swapped stories and yarns at the Hagerstown General Store. "Yes," he would say as he leaned back against Fred Johnson's counter, "my place is just about the right size. Twenty-five acres is big enough to support my family but not too big to handle." Of course, John Parker had a contrary opinion had he been allowed to voice it. To him, the farm was too large especially when he was dragooned into helping with the field chores such as plowing and weeding their corn, beans and tobacco crops.

John's family was about average for the era. He was the youngest of his three brothers and four sisters. His mother died giving birth to the youngest daughter when he was eight. His oldest brother Donald had little interaction with John who instead chose other diversions such as finding ways to escape the farm while chasing after the neighboring farm girls. John's oldest sister Margaret likewise had little interaction with him. After the death of their mother, Margaret became the *de facto* mother to the younger sisters and brothers. She did not care for the "assignment" but handled the job with as much energy, grace, and dedication as possible.

To be fair, John Parker did not have much interaction with his brothers and sisters except the normal family squabbles that occasionally erupted. John always raced them to the family table making sure he got his share of the meals and more if possible.

After his mother died, John quit school in the fourth grade. Had he voiced an opinion of his actions, he probably would have noted it had not been a great sacrifice for him. He was a poor student; his reading and writing skills were barely adequate to keep him from being classified as illiterate. Math was a great mystery to John, but he clung desperately to any money he might gain from the outside jobs he performed on rare occasions.

Around the time when John was fifteen (1845), he was introduced to another John – Mr. John Barleycorn. At first young Mr. Parker was revolted by the taste of the other John. The amber liquid felt like molten lead as it singed his tongue and attacked his throat on its way to his stomach. He remarked Mr. Barleycorn burned his "innards" for hours afterward.

As events sometimes tend to work themselves out, Parker grew more tolerant of the amber fire he consumed. His older brother and other lads from the area would sneak a bottle to his care from time to time. John developed a taste or immunity to Mr. Barleycorn's side effects. In fact, he became quite fond of his new friend's acquaintance that stayed with him throughout his life.

≈≈≈≈

John F. Parker was not charged with any crime or dereliction of duty during the investigation of the president's assassination. The Military Tribunal determined that he had discharged his official duties adequately on the night of April 14, 1865. He and other members of the Metropolitan Police Force had accompanied President Lincoln from the White House to Ford's Theater as prescribed which was the extent of their duties.

As a result of the publicity from the Military Tribunal's investigation, the public inferred that Parker had, in fact, failed in his duties to protect the president even if that were technically not true. Parker was only one person affected by the president's death. Among his police force colleagues and superiors, he was considered merely "adequate" as an officer. Parker's life-long affair with Mr. Barleycorn began to affect his work duties. In 1868 he was discharged from the Metropolitan Police Force for "violation of rules." The circumstances were hazy but whispered talk indicated Parker was increasingly too fond of the liquid fire he consumed.

From his discharge in 1868 to his death in 1890, Parker bounced among a series of menial jobs none of which he retained for any length of time. He died a poor man carrying an invisible and undeserved but real shroud of guilt with him.

≈≈≈≈

"Did you hear about John Parker?

"No, what happened?"

"He died last month from heart failure, I think, and was buried in the Pauper's Field outside town," replied Fred Johnson, a casual acquaintance of Parker's.

"Well, I hadn't seen him for months," said Richard Swensen, "he never seemed to shake the guilt that he drug around."

"Yeah, that was too bad," said Johnson, "I wonder how things would have turned out if Lincoln had lived?"

My Portrait

Lou Blazquez

"MAKE SURE YOU GET ALL THREE OF ME," I told the artist, who already had begun brushing across the canvas leaning on an easel. I mused as he worked.

One of us is a 10-year-old who gives me wonder, curiosity, mischievousness, and naiveté. He is simple in a complicated world, doesn't understand it, or America, or his house in which things disappear and are found again later. He asks, "Why can Gene Roddenberry figure out warp drive but not NASA?"

Another is a 16-year-old with uncertainty, self-consciousness, and self-doubt who fears failure more than anything. He has impatient youthful energy, and he is shy. He wants to say, "Bite me!" to anyone who angers him and then thrust a résumé of knuckles into their throats for future reference. But, he has black belt discipline and is thus harmless. He has a lust that began with the urge of mitosis three billion years ago and believes that the process was fun even then. That was why life began. When he makes intimate advances to women, he hates it when they ask him to control himself. "Why can't women show this fabulous self-control and *increase* their sex drive?"

I'm the elder, with the experience and wisdom of 59 years who must support the other two with food, shelter, movies, and dates. I'm the busy guy. I take mood disorder meds because my emotions can be overly capricious or confusing. I began a dedicated career of instructing children in 1972, but it's my daughter Jamie who is all-important. Teaching is what I do, a father is who I am.

Jamie displayed my 10-yearold self when she was four, walking her new puppy. A man was standing on his second story balcony when she called up to him, "Hey mister, do you want to pet my dog?" It made perfect sense, everyone was another her—is another me—and wanted to rush up to little Cinder and cuddle him.

The stranger called back, "No!"

"Okay," she replied brightly and happily moved on. I was puzzled with her cheerfulness at rejection. She knew something I didn't.

It took me a while to believe this, but I do now. In my life, I am allowed but one true relationship, and I had mine. My marriage changed me from an adult into a human being. Its ending is the biggest failure of my life because I grew up wanting one person, one family, and one trip to the altar. My ex-wife's friendship is still my North Star.

After my divorce, I accumulated ten parrots and a girlfriend named Robin. I stayed at her house in Mesa on weekends. When I had my only modeling gig, I got up extra early to allow for getting lost. I needed to shave closely, and I panicked when I realized I forgot my travel kit. Robin handed me a brand-new Bic plastic shaver. I lathered up and began. Nothing happened. I stroked harder, but my stubble stood firm. I couldn't press too hard, because I feared tracks of moist scabs on my face. Exasperated, I told Robin that the Bic didn't work. She was puzzled. My electric razor was the dismal solution.

I left her house, got lost, and arrived on time. I went to the woman who does make up for the agency. "Do you realize you have two different-colored socks? I'll tug your pants lower to cover them."

I got through the job for Reality Executives to their satisfaction. That night I was in bed with Robin. She jumped up and exclaimed, "Wait a minute!" and ran to the bathroom. There was uncontrolled laughter. She came back holding the Bic razor as if it were a scepter. While she was still hysterically shaking and choking, she took off its plastic top.

I asked, "What's that?"

"It's a protector."

"From what?"

"From cutting yourself."

"I want to be cut. That's how I get the whiskers off." She doubled over.

"What's so funny?" She knew something I didn't.

When she could finally speak, she told me I looked like a little boy, just lying there bewildered.

I wondered, how do I turn the comical into the romantic? I read, or maybe someone mentioned, that girls get turned on if you talk filthy to them in bed.

Youngsters—even when they're 59—will believe anything that adults tell them. In the dark, I whispered dirty words to Robin. She went into gyrations of hilarity. I like amusing people, even when it's unintentional, but I also like being in on the joke. "Now what?"

"That was like my little old grandmother cursing."

So much for advice and so much for obscenities. I should have known better because it wasn't natural. I try to be respectful, kind, and caring to the woman I'm with. It was always that way with Robin. After five minutes of unrestrained guffawing, she noticed me watching her without guile. With quiet intent, she suddenly embraced me. She never refused my fierce passion, loved my innocence, and appreciated my good sense. In moments, four hearts beat as one and three of them were mine.

There is the mire of my faults. I don't know how dark or how bad they can be; I've never been tested in my fortunate life. I have a distressing amount of cowardice, deceit, selfishness, laziness, crankiness, and vengefulness—wait! I changed my mind about that last one. Vengeful is good. I'm tired of the innocent getting kicked around. Hurt the bad guys. I have some cynicism, but not too much. Mankind is basically good. I am, too, but my worst side is the bad decisions I have made for my daughter and will never forgive myself. In my quiet moments, the wound still trickles. My flaws are there in despicable amounts. I am ashamed as the artist works uninterrupted. But if a man must have faults, what's wrong with mine? Mrs. Shannon said in *Night of the Iguana,* "Nothing human disgusts me unless it is unkind or violent." I hold her standards.

I wonder if other guys are like me. I don't know because I can only be one male at a time. It's hard to believe females can be like me. I've been close to those who have been bashed, treated like meat, have had long-term hurts, or had ex-husbands who steal their possessions. These women occasionally wanted fatherly moments recreated, being warmly held unconditionally, and just be touched with a subliminal healing without payoff and receive an occasional kiss on the forehead. I like being sensitive in those quiet moments. My partner briefly becomes a 10-year-old, as she deserves to be for the rest of her life. I can feel my adult nurturing and caring for her as we are silent in a different way.

Among the three of us, the consensus is that we are in the wrong reality. Our heaven and our good day are the same. Each morning I would be with a blonde, each afternoon I would be with my daughter, and at night, me and Roger Rabbit would shoot up Toon Town.

"Did you get us all?" I asked as the artist finished the last stroke. He turns the easel. I inhale.

Stirring the Memory

Judith A. Dempsey

A recent conversation with my baby brother Marty, who is in his seventies, brought to life some buried memories.

Lately, due to poor balance, I have experienced a series of falls. In the first fall I broke my left hip. In the second spill I broke my favorite angel statue. Then, I really hit the deck, all left side of me landed on the bathroom tile floor. At Sunday church several males suggested that I tell others, "You should see the other guy. Well not being a guy I prefer to just say, "I hit the deck, and this is the result."

Before retiring, my brother Marty was a county prosecutor in Ohio. He is very conscious of small details. Marty's next statement hit me right between the eyes. He said, "Judith, may now be a Dempsey but remember we are Aubry's and Aubry's tend to get in trouble."

How could I have forgotten some of the adventures my two brothers and I engaged in as children. I smiled at Marty and said "Really, still an Aubry?"

Then my mind started turning back to incidents of my childhood. As a young girl I had sticky hands, especially for chocolate bars that were not paid for. When a nun asked for flowers for the May altar, having none of our own, I stole Mrs. Treason's irises. Unfortunately, I dropped a few on my walk to school.

My older sister, Pauletta found them and reported the situation to Mom. Upon my arrival back home, Mom was waiting and told me in no uncertain terms I must go next door and confess my misdeed to Mrs. Theason and ask for forgiveness.

Once I told my story to Mrs. Theason, she bent down and gave me a hug for being so honest. Then to my surprise and delight she told me I could have as many irises as I wanted. I am now in my 80s and to this day I have irises in my yard.

As children, both of my younger brothers joined with me in raiding the alleys behind our home. I remember finding cast off lumber to build a play shed which we not only used for ourselves but shared with other neighborhood kids. We also used that rickety old shed as a place to hide when we needed to be alone.

Then there is the case of the sway back black sedan down the street from us. On a hot summer day, the three of us took a walk and stopped to watch a group of kids enjoying themselves sliding down the top of the car as if it were a slide. It looked like so much fun when they invited us to join them there was no hesitation on our part. However, it was not so much fun when our father asked if we had destroyed the neighbor's black sedan. We told our father that the other kids asked us to join them and they did the damage. It seems the other kids told their father it was the Aubry kids up the block who did the damage. I have no idea what our father had to pay for the damage that was caused but it was a lot and yes, we were sorely punished for our misdeed. We weren't bad kids, just active and imaginative. Yes, we Aubry's did get in trouble. But, for all the follies we committed, every one of us got advanced degrees and served society as adults: two attorneys, two counselors and one accountant. Yes, there were five of us. My two older sisters never got into as much trouble as my two younger brothers and me. At least, that's what our parents and our older sisters always told us.

Seven Hours Fine Except for Mothers

Dolores Comeaux-Everard

London psychiatrist Jane Gomer believes "too much rest can shorten your life." The author of "How Not to Die Young" suggests that seven hours or less of sleep is ideal.

What a heavenly hypothesis for new mothers who practice demand feedings, and late-night TV addicts. Wide-eyed sufferers can now boast rather than curse insomnia.

Last week I had a bout with inadvertent insomnia. The symptoms became acute. A look in the mirror set off a chorus of high-pitched voices chanting, "ring-around-the-eyeballs."

A family health guide says abnormal wakefulness can be caused by poor sleeping conditions. Noise, light, someone moving around and worries are all indicative of the ailment.

The problem began at about 1:30 a.m. on Saturday when my husband began pacing the floor in anticipation for our daughter's cast party being held after the production of "Fiddler on the Roof."

Probing real and imagined fears, we discussed everything from wrecks and abductions to crazy snipers lurking on the highway. The talk proved a catharsis for him but not for me. Twenty minutes passed before the car bumped up the drive. Our Cinderella entered to a round of parental applause.

By 2 a.m., I gave in to saucer-sized eyes and trudged toward the typewriter where I pecked away until my peepers pooped. The vigil led to a sluggish next morning. No sooner did my head hit the pillow that night than Z's began dancing.

A rapping at the front door stifled my slumber. I pried open sleepy eyes to note the digital clock was blinking a hazy 5 a.m. As I dragged my body aft, I wondered why the "Gestapo" was in my town. I remembered voting in Saturday's primary, but only once. Yesterday when the children burst two bean bag chairs that released trillions of polystyrene beads in the house, I threatened to kill them, but thoughts don't equal deeds.

Clad in a nightgown, I crouched behind the banging door then slowly opened it. As laser beam struck my terror-filled eyes. Shielding my face from the flashlight, I recognized the "storm troopers" to be the new milkman and his wife. To guarantee future delivery, they explained, I must pay our overdue bill.

As I searched for a checkbook, I wondered what company psychologist had drummed up this choice piece of behavior modification.

"When and how do we get bills?" I queried.

"Oh, we slap them on the milk bottle, the couple answered.

That explains it. One of our boys has the job of bringing in the milk. Sometimes he becomes engrossed in early morning cartoons, and he forgets about his job until returning from school by which time the milk has soured. There was no doubt in my mind that the bill had met its fate fluttering about in the dawn dew.

Back in bed, my drowsy husband interrogated me about the knocking.

"Oh, go back to sleep…that commotion was only Elmer and Elsie hoofing-it-up over some green stuff."

Angel Fish, Guppies & Tetras!
Oh My!

John Maher

THE OLD MAN OPPOSED GIVING weekly allowances to his three sons. He regarded the practice as anathema, an absolute mortal sin, the product of misguided followers of the Dr. Spock spare-the-rod school of parenting. He believed in the tenet that nobody gave you anything. If you wanted or needed something, then you worked for it through hard labor. You earned your keep. He based this conviction on the hardships of his childhood as the oldest of four siblings of Irish immigrant parents. His father died at 39 years of age, leaving The Old Man the designated head of the house and chief breadwinner at age ten.

With this as a fixed parental principle, my older brother Tom and I made money by mowing neighbors' lawns and shoveling snow from their driveways. I was six and Tom ten when we started doing this. Tom also had a newspaper route delivering Newsday, the leading daily Long Island rag. At nine, I took over his route. I had my own "walking around money," as my father called it. Most of what I made I saved to buy Christmas and birthday presents for my family. In hindsight, making my own money gave me a sense of independence and accomplishment at an early age. But, at the time I detested it and felt different from my friends and classmates who mostly got everything they wanted.

At some point, I decided I wanted to spend some of my cash on a tropical fish aquarium. Thinking about it now, I can't recall my motivation. My brothers and I weren't into nature or science; we focused on sports. It might have been that one of my friends had an aquarium and having one represented an acceptance thing. At any rate, when I told my mother, she was thrilled, which surprised me, because I expected significant pushback on the idea. Over the years, we had had about a half dozen goldfish swimming in little glass bowls. Added to this were many baby chicks and little bunnies in cardboard boxes, all of them acquired as Easter presents. The Old Man assigned my brother and me personal care for these poor creatures. Like kids our age, we paid attention to our duties for, oh, I don't know, 15 or 20 minutes. Then sometime later the animals croaked and promptly departed for God's Big Pet Cemetery in the sky. Mom cleaned up the mess and performed the burial services on our pet boot hill in the backyard.

So, my mother's positive reaction to my announced entrance into the study of marine biology came as a shock. She was overjoyed with the notion which was out of character. Mom could be a Pollyanna, but she reserved most of her excitement for her daily 4 o'clock silver bullet cocktails, martinis ("It's time. The sun is over the yardarm.") and dinner parties. Mom saw herself as a cross between Auntie Mame and the Unsinkable Molly Brown. And she loved Ethel Merman, baby.

Riding this wave of enthusiasm, we drove to the local pet store. I bought a 10-gallon tank. To make it an aquarium, I added rocks, underwater plastic plants and multicolored gravel to spread along the bottom. A miniature deep-sea diver attached to a filter to keep it clean. And a partially submerged glass heating tube, which contained heating coils to maintain the correct temperature. I also bought a fluorescent light that sat on the tank top and a long-handled wire fishnet to catch the four guppies I purchased, the cheapest fish available.

We put the tank, its components, and the four prized inhabitants on the kitchen counter between the breadbox and the three round ceramic canisters filled with flour, sugar and tea bags. That way Mom could look at the fish. It lasted there a week until she banished it to the den because of the filter's annoying hum and fishy odors.

Moving the tank was no simple task. Filled with 10 gallons of water, it weighed over eighty pounds, but my older brother, Mom and I repositioned it without incident.

The den, also known as the TV room but never called that, was my brothers' and my special domain. At one time, it had been a screened-in porch on the side of the house connected by a single French door to the living room. After the birth of my younger brother Patrick, my parents converted the porch into a place where they could park three young boys. With the door closed, we'd be practically unheard during those infrequent times we were allowed in the house, which was in keeping with my Mother's principle that "children should be seen and not heard." (And the seeing part should be limited.) If we weren't outside playing or upstairs in our rooms either doing homework or sleeping, we were in the den watching TV with the door closed.

The den was a 12′ x 15′ room with windows on three sides, pine-paneled walls, a low white acoustic tile ceiling and a dark speckled linoleum floor. Built-in shelves along one wall held books and my parent's record collection of 1940s 78s and the newer 1950s 33⅓ LPs. Mom decorated with an uncomfortable, torturous-to-sleep on gray Castro Convertible couch and two bent rattan armchairs and matching ottoman featuring ugly flowered cushions.

We placed the tropical fish tank along the den's long wall under the two windows that faced the side lawn. It sat on a black metal coffee cart that Mom had picked up at E. J. Korvettes, a new discount store on the Manhasset's Miracle Mile. Like much of Korvettes' merchandise, the coffee cart, a splendid example of Japan's 1950s industrial recovery, was seemingly produced from old Budweiser beer cans, unused Zero airplane rivets, and wobbly white plastic casters. It was bargain-basement and flimsy beyond description, but it conformed to my mother's economic doctrine of squeezing a buck until the eagle shit. She hated buying anything from Japan, those sneaky Oriental bastards had attacked Pearl Harbor, but she couldn't resist the price.

While Mom was untutored about interior design, she had even less knowledge about metal fabrication, manufacturing tolerances, and gravity. She had an associate degree in home economics from Pratt Institute that taught her to cook for 300 hospital patients but not for a family of five. Unfortunately, her course of study did not cover structural engineering or metallurgy. Although the black metal coffee cart appeared stable enough to bear a load of cups, saucers, plates, flatware, and cookies, it wasn't designed to support a tropical fish tank with 80+ pounds of water. But it proved an adequate platform for the tank so long as it remained stationary.

Over the course of the next few months, I added to the four-guppy fish community. I invested my newspaper route earnings in zebras, red mollies, silver tetras, blue bettas, striped angelfish, and a bottom feeder that looked like a little catfish. I bought two of each fish because I assumed they'd want company and anyway Noah had two of each on the Ark. I didn't get a second small catfish. It was too ugly.

A curious development took place. The more fish I brought home, the more enthusiastic my mother became about the fish tank. As her interest and involvement grew, mine faded, not because she was butting into my hobby, but because I was a 10-year-old kid with a limited attention span.

As I moved on to buying my first boat, Mom took over the care and feeding of the fish. Almost every day, she would appear in the den, turn on the fluorescent light, and sprinkle fish flakes on the surface of the water. Then she'd gaze on the different pairs of fish as they bobbed and weaved for the floating food and speak to them because she had named them. At one point, the guppies had babies. Mom was over the moon… until a day later when she noticed that most of the fry had disappeared and realized someone in the tank was a cannibal. Crestfallen, this provided reason enough to have an early martini.

Disaster struck one Sunday afternoon. The Old Man was out of town on business and Mom was visiting neighbors two houses down the street. Tom, Patrick and I were in the den engrossed in the NFL football contest between our team, the New York Giants and the hated Cleveland Browns. As the game wore on, we reenacted plays from the game. Patrick would try to run the ball like Cleveland's famed running back Jim Brown. Tom would tackle him like Sam Huff, the Giants all-pro middle linebacker. And I would jump on top of both like Andy Robustelli, the Giants star defensive end.

This activity meant our bodies were flying around. The Castro convertible got most of the abuse and the bent rattan chairs, and its ugly cushions were strewn about in various directions. Then, it happened. The ottoman was pushed violently with a dull thud against the black metal coffee cart holding the fish tank. We stopped and watched transfixed. It drifted shakily along the wall on its spindly plastic caster wheels. Then it wobbled in slow motion back and forth, the to and fro movement speeding up as the wave action increased in the tank. The tank swayed like a metronome until the cart collapsed to the linoleum floor with a loud, wet thunk.

In seconds the three of us were standing there speechless, wild-eyed, mouths agape, our feet submerged in a three-inch pond of fish tank water that covered the linoleum floor. The flood was up to the doorsill leading into the living room. But there was no seepage out. Fish wiggled everywhere.

Maggie our pit bull barked once at the flopping fish and bolted from the room. As Patrick giggled at the sight, I intoned in a paralyzed state the proper invocation of "Ohmygod! Ohmygod!" Ohmygod! Ohmygod!" Then my older brother Tom, the family's designated manager-in-waiting and most cool-headed of the three of us, yelled, "STOP! Get the buckets out in the garage and grab the mop and sponges in the kitchen! GO!" Then he turned around and threw open the two windows along the wall that faced the side lawn.

Patrick and I returned to the den with the buckets, sponges, and mop and stood there dumbfounded with our mouths opened. Tom snatched a bucket out of my semi-paralyzed hand and scooped up water with abandon, tossing it out the windows onto the rose bushes and the side lawn. Recognizing a brilliant idea,

Patrick and I joined in, bailing the fish tank water out the window like desperate men trying to save a sinking boat.

At some point in the operation, I said to Tom, "What about the fish?" My fish were still flopping on the floor albeit with declining vigor. "Johnny, they're goners. Scoop 'em up and put 'em in the bucket." I took the long wire-handled fishnet, and downhearted picked up my bettas and tetras and guppies and mollies and the lovely elegant striped angelfish. I placed them lovingly in a bucket. Then Tom and I gave them a burial at sea. We flushed them down the toilet.

We dried the floor with rolls of paper towels and put the furniture back in its exact place. We found the coffee cart hadn't broken. It had collapsed under the shifting weight of the water, which caused its shelves to rotate on the rivets that held them to the frame. Once pulled back upright, it looked fine, except for bent metal on the corners. We were even luckier to find that the glass on three of the four sides intact, except on the back side. It had cracked and given way when the tank hit the floor. We set it back on the cart, gathered up and put the multicolored gravel, rocks, and underwater plants back on the bottom of the tank rearranged the filter and heater unit and put the fluorescent light back on the top. Then we sited the tank and cart as it had looked. Once accomplished, we went back to watching what remained of the football game. When Mom came home, we were all smiles.

Tuesday night, two evenings later I was upstairs in "the boy's room," pretending to do my homework when I heard my mother's muffled scream from the den. I knew what was coming. Ten seconds later, she screeched up the stairs, "John!" What's interesting, she didn't call for her cherubic younger son Patrick the comedian of the family, or her older son Tommy, the paragon of virtue, the golden child. Oh no, it was the middle one, the one who was always causing trouble. She was beside herself. "How could you?"

I was uncertain about her being upset. Was it because we broke the tank? Or was it because when she went to feed the fish, the fish flakes didn't float on the surface of the water, but instead. they fluttered down to the tank bottom like snowflakes. At any rate, after trying to explain what happened without success, she gave me the ultimate rebuke, "Wait 'til your father gets home."

When The Old Man returned from his business trip, and I had to face the consequences, rather than taking my head off figuratively and literally, he was reserved. I chalked it up to fatigue from the trip. I was word-whipped for my stupidity and for upsetting my mother.

But since I had wasted my own money, he concluded I was just a nitwit. The fish tank, its accessories, and the black metal coffee cart got parked out in the garage to gather dust.

Thirty years later, my brothers and I were having an infrequent dinner with The Old Man. He and Mom separated twenty years previously, their divorce lasting longer than the Vietnam War and bloodier. Tom reminisced about the fish tank episode, which by this time had become a featured and hilarious recollection for the three of us. Much to our surprise, The Old Man laughed and said, "God damn, that was funny what you did to your mother. I had a lot of trouble keeping it together when I had to scold you for it. That was really funny."

Mom, of course, never saw anything funny about the event.

The End

Reading gives us someplace to go when we have to stay where we are.

— Mason Cooley (1927-2002)

About The Authors

The authors who comprise the group known as AZ WRITERS are talented and serious writers from all parts of the globe. They are lesser-known authors who like to write and share their work with others. The only requirements to becoming a part of this group is being able to put together an interesting story that you would like to share with others.

If you have short story that fits the parameters, and you are a decent writer please feel free to contact our staff at:

yourazwriters@gmail.com

***

Two Photos, one for each of my Gemini Personalities.

As for the compiler, editor, formatter, and publisher of the AZ Writers Short Story and Poetry Anthologies . . .

Pat Fogarty is an editor, award-winning author, and poet. Born and raised in the South Bronx, his works are infused with personal experiences. He writes Creative Non-fiction, and literary fiction novels, Pat also writes short stories and poems; many of which have been published in a plethora of magazines and journals—locally, nationally, and internationally.

His short stories have also been included in several anthologies. Pat is the Editor & Publisher of the AZ Writers Best Short Stories, Best Poems, Best New Short Stories, & Best New Poetry series. Pat retired from the International Brotherhood of Electrical Workers in 2005 after 35 years of service. He is also an accredited Alcohol and Substance Abuse Counselor as well as a Certified Union Counselor. He is currently the President of The Central Arizona Writers and past president of the Professional Writers of Prescott. Pat is happily married to his soul-mate Susan, and together they enjoy spending time at their home in the Mountains of Central Arizona with their German Shepherd Dog and three Irish Terriers.

www.ingramcontent.com/pod-product-compliance
Lightning Source LLC
Chambersburg PA
CBHW080907190726
48294CB00008B/1993
9781732812130